A Time of Innocence

A Time of Innocence

Warren Burke

Walker and Company
New York

Copyright © 1986 Matt Braun

All rights reserved. No part of this book may be reproduced or transmitted in any form or by any means, electric or mechanical, including photocopying, recording, or by any information storage and retrieval system, without permission in writing from the Publisher.

All the characters and events portrayed in this story are fictitious.

First published in the United States of America in 1986 by the Walker Publishing Company, Inc.

Published simultaneously in Canada by John Wiley & Sons Canada, Limited, Rexdale, Ontario.

Library of Congress Cataloging-in-Publication Data

Braun, Matthew.
   A time of innocence.

   I. Title
PS3552.R355T56   1986   813'.54   86-1585
ISBN 0-8027-0888-9

Book design by Irwin Wolf

Printed in the United States of America

10 9 8 7 6 5 4 3 2 1

PROLOGUE

Untold until now, *A Time of Innocence* is a true story. Like all fiction based on fact, certain liberties have been taken with characters and events. Yet the essential elements are accurate in every respect.

A family of spies was instrumental in the success of the attack on Pearl Harbor. All were trained operatives, clandestine German agents on loan to the Japanese. One of them was young and beautiful, skilled in the art of seduction and intelligence gathering. She was the catalyst in all that transpired on the morning of December 7, 1941.

A Time of Innocence is her story.

Warren Burke
July 10, 1985

A Time of Innocence

1

TOM GORDON COULDN'T wait to see her. All day she'd been the only thing on his mind. In fact, he had been thinking about her for the past month. A long, monkish month at sea.

Whistling tunelessly under his breath, Gordon disengaged the clutch and downshifted into second gear. The Ford coupe groaned, then took the steep incline with a surge of power. The road climbed steadily upward through the terraced streets of Halawa Heights.

Nowhere on Oahu was there a more commanding vista. To the north, the slopes of the Koolau Range loomed against a darkening sky. Below, along the southern shoreline, Pearl Harbor was ringed with lights. Some seven miles upcoast, the neon blaze of downtown Honolulu was visible. Dwarfing all else, like some magical backdrop, the opalescent waters of the Pacific swept endlessly to the horizon. It was a view that only the very wealthy could afford.

Gordon turned left on Manaiki Drive. The last house on the block was a palatial stone structure with white, stucco walls and terra-cotta tiled roof. Built on an oblique angle, it occupied the whole of a broad cul-de-sac. An upper story at the far end of the house abutted the mountainside. The lower floor was shaded by a Chinese banyan tree, and exotic flowers bordered the carefully manicured lawn. A Cadillac sedan, ivory with chocolate brown interior, sat in the driveway. Gordon pulled in and braked to a halt. He killed the coupe's engine.

Stepping from the car, he tugged a naval officer's cap down over his eyes. Beneath sandy hair, his features were pleasant, lightly peppered with freckles. The trim fit of his dress white uniform indicated he kept himself in shape. On the porch, he pressed the door buzzer. A footstep sounded inside and the door opened. The man who greeted him spoke in heavily accented English.

"Lieutenant Gordon. How nice to see you again."

"Good evening, Dr. Hahn."

"Won't you come in."

"Thank you." Gordon removed his cap. "I believe Susan is expecting me."

"Of course. Shall we wait in the living room?"

Eric Hahn led the way with a brisk, determined stride. He was distinguished in bearing, always impeccably dressed. His hair was flecked with gray, and though he was approaching fifty, he looked ten years younger.

"May I offer you a drink, Lieutenant?"

"I . . . " Gordon checked his watch.

"Plenty of time," Hahn assured him. "Women believe clocks were invented for men. I fear the axiom applies equally to my daughter."

Gordon laughed politely. "A short one, then."

"Gin and tonic, as I recall."

"Yes, thank you."

"Perhaps Mama will join us."

"How is Mrs. Hahn?"

"Excellent, never better. She will be delighted to see you."

Upstairs, Susan sat before the vanity table in her bedroom. Her makeup, almost complete, accentuated the exquisite bone structure of her face. She finished applying a pale mauve eye shadow. Then, her head angled critically, she examined the results in the vanity table mirror. Parted at the center, her thick, sable hair hung loose, turning under in a soft curl where it touched her shoulders. Deep violet eyes provided a striking contrast with her creamy complexion and sparkled with approval. She thought mauve, which complimented her outfit for tonight, added just the right touch. She looked mysterious, somehow unattainable.

Satisfied, she stood and shrugged out of her housecoat. For her height, almost five four in heels, she was perfectly proportioned. Her effect on men was something she'd learned to accept—and play on. She was, by turn, darkly vivacious, vulnerable, and a creature of bewitching sensuality. She sometimes felt older than her twenty-one years, much older.

From the closet, she took a crepe de Chine evening skirt. Banded at the waist, the skirt was dusky ultramarine with a slit up the side. The companion top was a skimpy swath of cloth, dyed a luscious shade of teal. A simple halter, it was wrapped from behind, crisscrossed over the front, and tied around the neck. Her midriff and shoulders, not to mention most of her back, were bare. She added earrings, a bracelet, and a flawless sapphire on her ring hand. She then moved to a full-length mirror.

The effect was stunning. She couldn't decide whether she looked half-dressed or half-undressed. Either way, it would create a sensation at the Officers' Club. Few of the naval wives would realize she was wearing the fashion hit of 1941, perfectly in vogue. Instead, green with envy, they would attempt to keep their husbands from staring too openly. She knew already that it would be a losing battle. And she found the whole idea vastly appealing. She enjoyed being the center of attention.

As she started toward the bedroom door, her thoughts turned to Tom Gordon. Not for the first time, a nagging question crossed her mind. She wondered how she might avoid going to bed with him tonight. That too, she concluded, was a losing battle.

* * *

"Another drink, Lieutenant?"

"No, I'm fine, Mrs. Hahn. Thanks anyway."

Gordon was seated in an overstuffed armchair. Greta Hahn and her husband were across from him on the sofa. Watching her now, Gordon was struck again by the dissimilarity between mother and daughter. She was in her early forties, plump and large busted, her hair pulled back in a severe bun. Everyone's caricature of the typical German hausfrau. He marveled that she had produced a daughter like Susan. It hardly seemed in the genes.

"Are you eating properly?" Greta inquired.

Her non sequitur took Gordon by surprise. "Pardon me?"

"You're much too thin." Greta clucked and shook her head maternally. "Do they feed you enough on that . . . what was the word you used?"

"A pigboat."

"Pigboat." Greta made a face. "The word alone ruins your appetite. I must ask Susan to bring you home to dinner some night. Young men need to eat properly."

"Yes, ma'am! Anytime you say. I never turn down a home cooked meal."

Gordon was executive officer on a submarine. His ship, the *Dolphin*, had returned from a long patrol only day before yesterday. His last date with Susan had been almost a month ago. He was somewhat flattered that her mother remembered his assignment, took such an interest. All the more so since Susan dated several officers besides himself. He felt singled out.

Gordon was also impressed for an altogether different reason. He thought it remarkable that the Hahns had become Americanized in such a short period of time. According to scuttlebutt, the family had fled Germany in 1937. He recalled hearing, as well, that their flight was prompted by religious problems.

Hitler was persecuting Jews, and there was speculation that Dr. Hahn was part Jewish. Gordon knew nothing of Jews, or their religious beliefs. Nor was he all that familiar with the manners and customs of Germans. Yet he was thoroughly impressed by what he'd seen of the Hahn family thus far. They were high-class people and at the same time very down-to-earth. The fact that they were obviously quite wealthy made it all the more remarkable. They never put on grand airs or acted the least bit pretentious. They were just themselves.

"Hello everyone."

Susan swept into the living room. She was a vision of loveliness, and Gordon hastily got to his feet as she entered. The light evening wrap thrown over her shoulders did nothing to hide her exposed look.

"Wow," Gordon mumbled.

"Do you like it?" she inquired innocently. "I wasn't sure whether it was appropriate for the Officers' Club."

"You'll knock their eyes out."

"Oh, Tom. You really are a flatterer."

She moved across the room. Her father rose from the sofa and she kissed him on the cheek. "Good evening, Papa."

"Lieutenant Gordon is right. You look charming, my dear."

"You approve, then?"

"I do indeed."

"I'm glad."

"Enjoy yourselves," Hahn said, "and don't be too late."

Susan darted him a look. Then she turned to Gordon with a warm smile. "Shall we go?"

"You bet."

"Good night, Mama."

She linked her arm to his, hugging it to her. He flushed and his freckles turned a livid strawberry red. On the way out the door he called over his shoulder.

"Night, Dr. Hahn, night, Mrs. Hahn."

"Good night, Lieutenant."

Hahn waited until he heard the front door close. Then he walked to the far side of the room, where French doors opened onto a flagstone patio, and went outside.

The patio overlooked a sheer drop-off at the rear of the house, and afforded a panoramic view of Pearl Harbor and the ocean beyond. The lights of the naval base flickered with erratic brilliance, not quite a mile below Halawa Heights. Hahn stopped at a stone railing on the edge of the patio, his hands clasped behind his back. He stared down through the deepening night for a long while. His gaze was fixed on Pearl Harbor.

2

THE OFFICERS' CLUB was always mobbed for Saturday night's dinner dance, which featured a full orchestra. Tonight the crowd was in particularly festive spirits.

On the mainland that afternoon, the Annapolis football team had soundly trounced its opponent. Except for a handful of reservists, the officers stationed at Pearl Harbor were graduates of the Naval Academy. So an air of celebration and boisterous good humor pervaded the club. Loud cheers went up whenever the orchestra broke out in the Annapolis fight song.

Kathryn Ordway was one of the more exurberant rooters. Her father was Vice Admiral Thomas Ordway, class of '04. She prided herself on being a navy brat, and the daughter of Pearl Harbor's second in command. Moreover, her date tonight was Commander John Forster. He was class of '23 and chief of Naval Intelligence for the Pacific Fleet. She thought it ample reason to take the floor and exhort the crowd. She led every cheer with zesty, schoolgirl abandon.

Forster watched her antics with an indulgent smile. She was blond and tawny, a statuesque young woman with long lissome legs and high rounded breasts, bright eyes and a quick smile. She was surpassingly attractive. He had only one regret, and that was her age.

Kathryn was twenty-four while he was pushing forty. That,

added to the fact that he was divorced, presented what seemed an insurmountable problem. Her father was immovable on the subject of their marriage, refusing all discussion. The matter was further complicated by the fleet chain of command. Forster reported directly to Admiral Ordway.

The orchestra segued from the Academy fight song into a swing number. Kathryn sat down, her face flushed with excitement. She took a long thirsty drink of her Salty Dog. The icy blend of grapefruit juice and gin made her shudder.

"Whew, I needed that!"

"Cheerleading is hard work," Forster deadpanned.

"Is that a compliment or a wisecrack?"

"You can pep up my football team anytime."

"Funny man." Kathryn looked toward the foyer. "Where in the world is Susan? She's almost an hour late."

They were seated at a table for four. Kathryn had insisted on delaying dinner until Susan arrived. She considered Susan her best friend, her confidante. Forster was somewhat less enthusiastic about the relationship.

"Susan's always late," he noted dryly. "How else would she make her grand entrance?"

"Don't be catty, Commander."

"Who, me?"

Kathryn stared at him, thoughtful. He was a man of saturnine good looks and a strong, determined face. His voice was deep and resonant, and he was surprisingly gentle in their more intimate moments. Yet she sometimes thought his work in counterespionage made him too cynical. It was a trait that bothered her.

"Aren't you being a tad unkind?"

"No," he said with a half smile. "In fact, she's about to prove my point."

The orchestra paused between numbers. A sudden hush fell over the crowd and everyone seemed to turn in unison. Susan stood poised in the doorway, her hand tucked in Gordon's arm. The evening wrap was off her shoulders, revealing the swell of her breasts through the halter. Several women gasped, and every man in the room stared at her with undisguised admiration. She smiled serenely, leading the way to the table with her head arched high. She waited for Gordon to hold her chair, then sat down.

"Sorry we're late," she apologized. "I had a terrible time deciding what to wear."

"God, Susan!" Kathryn laughed out loud. "You're a riot."

"Why not? It'll give the old biddies something to talk about over dessert. Good evening, John."

"Susan." Forster looked faintly amused. He turned to Gordon. "How are things on the *Dolphin*, Lieutenant?"

Gordon still hadn't recovered from the entrance. His freckles betrayed his embarrassment. "Fine, sir. Out and back, strictly a routine patrol."

"You look like you could stand a drink."

"I sure could, Commander. A double."

Some while later, the orchestra played Glenn Miller's arrangement of "Sunrise Serenade." Susan and Gordon joined the rush to the dance floor. Forster offered Kathryn a cigarette, then took one himself and produced a lighter. Kathryn smoked in silence a moment.

"Have you ever noticed?" she mused. "Susan really is a marvelous dancer. She's very graceful."

"What I noticed," he remarked, "was her outfit. The boys at the bar look like they're ready to start shouting, 'Take it off!'"

Kathryn angrily puffed smoke. "Everyone at Pearl is stuck in a rut. And that goes especially for women!"

"Maybe that's why you don't have any friends . . . except Susan."

"What a horrible thing to say! I have tons and tons of friends."

"Where are they?" Forster smiled ruefully. "We always sit with Susan and her date. No one else has joined our table in months. Why is that?"

"You're so smart, you tell me."

"Susan," he said simply. "She's pure poison to other women."

"She's part Jewish," Kathryn sniffed. "That's the real reason. Common, ordinary prejudice! And I think it's disgusting."

"You're wrong, Kate. She's a threat to every woman on the base—married or otherwise."

One of the officers at the bar stood apart from the others. His shoulder boards indicated he was a lieutenant commander, and the expression on his face indicated he preferred the company of women to men. He slowly swigged a scotch on the rocks and watched Susan.

A tall man, his features were rugged and tanned. His eyes were a piercing blue, and a shock of tousled blond hair spilled down over his forehead. His smile was lazy, almost ironic, and there was an enormous air of confidence about him. He looked like a man accustomed to getting his own way.

As the orchestra went into a medley, he tossed off his scotch and turned from the bar. He moved to the dance floor, threading a path through the couples and approached Susan and Gordon, who were cheek to cheek in a close embrace. He tapped Gordon on the shoulder.

"Mind if I cut in, old man?"

Gordon looked up, startled. "Why—"

"Thanks ever so much."

He swept Susan out of Gordon's arms and glided her away in perfect tempo to the music. She had the impression of a man who was devastatingly handsome, and an absolute menace to virgins. He grinned down at her with the bold assurance of a pirate.

"I'm Harry Bendix."

"How nice," she said sweetly. "Are you in the habit of kidnapping strange young women, Mr. Bendix?"

"Only when her name is Susan Hahn."

"We haven't met before, have we?"

"Nope." His smile widened. "I asked your name at the bar."

"Did you? May I inquire why?"

"I'm new to Pearl. Only arrived a couple of days ago."

"I fail to see the connection."

"I don't know anyone here and you're the prettiest girl in the club. I always start at the top of the list."

"Well—" Susan's laugh was a delicious sound. "I must say you have quite a line, Mr. Bendix."

"Call me Harry. All my friends do."

"Are we going to be friends . . . Harry?"

Bendix winked. "We already are."

He pulled her close and smoothly whirled her away.

"See what I mean?"

Forster pointed a finger at Susan. By comparison, the other women on the dance floor looked rather dowdy. What was worse, they knew that their husbands and boyfriends were mentally making the same comparison. It seemed somehow unfair, an uneven contest.

"Watch their faces," Forster said. "They think she's a cross between Jezabel and a femme fatale. In short, they'd like to gouge her eyes out."

"Well, what of it?" Kathryn demanded. "It's just spite! They're envious of her, that's all."

"Maybe—" Forster suddenly stopped. "Well, would you look at that."

"What?"

"She's dancing with Harry Bendix."

"Who's Harry Bendix?"

"The slickest ladies' man ever to graduate from Annapolis. Wise men hide their daughters when he hits the fleet."

Kathryn turned in her chair. Her eyes narrowed and she studied the man who held Susan. She had the sinking sensation that she was watching a hunter stalk his prey.

On the dance floor, Bendix seemed to devour Susan with his eyes. He held her with one arm around her waist, his hand touching her bare back. The warmth of her body and the light scent of her perfume were like an aphrodisiac. His smile was almost immoral, his voice a caress.

"Kismet was kind on this assignment."

"Oh, how so?"

"If I hadn't been sent to Pearl, I wouldn't have met you."

Her throaty laughter floated over the dance floor. "Do you flirt with all the girls so shamelessly?"

"No, I'm serious," he said with a rougish grin. "I believe kismet shapes people's lives. We were fated to meet."

"And where did kismet transfer you from, Harry?"

"Long Beach. I got a promotion and a new assignment all the same day."

"How marvelous!"

"Yeah, it really was my lucky day. I didn't know how much so . . . till I saw you."

"Behave yourself," she scolded. "Tell me about your new assignment. What ship are you on?"

"The *Nevada*," he said importantly. "Top battlewagon in the fleet. I'm the new gunnery officer."

"You sound pleased."

"Am I ever! Nobody makes flag rank unless they've served aboard a battleship."

"Then you hope to be an admiral some day?"

"Like I said, kismet's on my side."

The orchestra finished the last number in the medley. Bendix reluctantly saw her back to her table. He exchanged pleasantries with Forster and was introduced to Kathryn. As he turned away, Gordon approached from the direction of the bar. Bendix grinned like a cat spitting feathers.

Gordon gave him a dirty look.

The Officers' Club closed at midnight. Kathryn and Forster said goodbye outside and walked off toward the far end of the parking lot. Susan waved to them, then went along with Gordon to his coupe. In the car, she settled back against the seat and awaited the inevitable.

Gordon climbed in on the driver's side. He shut the door and leaned across the seat. His breath smelled of whiskey and stale tobacco. He kissed her hard on the mouth.

"How about a drive to the beach?"

"What happened to your friend's apartment?"

"Bad timing. His ship's in port, too."

"Oh, Tom."

"C'mon, have a heart. I've been out to sea almost a month."

"Well, okay. But just this once, Tom Gordon. Next time you make arrangements with your friend."

"I promise. Cross my heart and Scout's honor."

Gordon started the engine. He rammed the gear shift into low and drove out of the parking lot. Susan slumped against the seat and exhaled a long sigh. Her head turned toward the window, her gaze fixed on the starry sky. She tried not to think about the beach.

3

IT WAS HALF past two in the morning when Susan entered the study. She wore a housecoat and her face looked freshly scrubbed. Her expression was calm, almost stoic. She sat quietly in a wing chair.

Hahn, seated behind the desk, ignored her. Arranged before him were a fountain pen and a leather-bound journal. He put on a pair of reading glasses and uncapped the fountain pen. In a precise hand, he entered the date in the journal. He then glanced up at Susan.

"Let us proceed. The subject of tonight's report is Lieutenant Thomas Gordon. His ship is the U.S.S. *Dolphin*."

Susan made no comment. She waited as he jotted down the information, writing in German. He peered at her over his glasses.

"Aside from Gordon, who were your companions tonight?"

"Commander John Forster and Kathryn Ordway."

"Any other contacts?"

"No—" She stopped abruptly. "Yes, there was one other. A Lieutenant Commander Harry Bendix. I danced with him once."

"Who is he?"

"The new gunnery officer on the *Nevada*. He's just been assigned to the fleet."

"Where was his last assignment?"

"The naval base at Long Beach, California."

"Why did you dance only once with Bendix?"

"Tom Gordon became very jealous. I had no wish to make him angry — and uncooperative."

Hahn reflected a moment. "We will return to Bendix later. For now, let us concentrate on Gordon. Please begin."

The debriefing went quickly. Hahn listened, prompting her with questions, and entered it all in the journal. Susan spoke as though quoting things committed to memory. Her voice was without inflection.

"Eight submarines are in port at present. Six are operational and two are in dry dock for repairs."

"Has the number of subs operating out of Pearl Harbor been changed?"

She shook her head. "It remains the same, twenty-two."

"You mentioned subs in dry dock. What is the nature of the repairs?"

"Their new sonar equipment has problems. In Gordon's words, they have to work the 'bugs' out."

"Did he elaborate on the problem?"

"No."

"Has it occurred in all the subs?"

"Yes, at one time or another. But he feels the problem will be corrected quite shortly. I gather the navy doesn't consider it a major hindrance."

"So we can reliably report that the sonar capability is functional?"

"Overall that would be correct."

"What else?"

"The navy now has approximately a hundred of the new Balao class submarines. Gordon wasn't sure of the exact number because it's top secret. But he does know that one-third of the force operates in the Pacific."

"With the balance assigned to the Atlantic Fleet?"

"He drew that conclusion from scuttlebutt, rumors."

"Were you able to obtain further details about the Balao class subs?"

"Nearly everything," she said impassively. "The range, without refueling, is ten thousand miles at surface speed. Maximum surface speed is twenty-one knots, reduced to nine knots when submerged."

"How long can the ship remain submerged?"

"Up to twenty-four hours. Then they must surface and recharge the batteries. Usually it takes four to six hours for the diesel engines to complete a full recharge."

Hahn jotted it all down. "How deep can the ship dive?"

"Between four and five hundred feet. Gordon said the maximum depth would be attempted only in an emergency."

"Such as an attack by enemy destroyers?"

"Yes."

"What surveillance equipment does the ship carry?"

"On the surface, it uses air search radar and radio intercept. Submerged, it relies on sonar and sound listening devices."

"You are certain about the radar?"

"I'm certain that Gordon mentioned it."

"Excellent!" Hahn scribbled furiously. "This is the first indication we've had of air search radar on submarines."

"Is that meaningful?"

"Oh, indeed. It greatly enhances a sub's offensive capability on the surface. Were you able to determine the number of torpedoes carried?"

"Ten firing tubes and twenty-four torpedoes."

"Anything else?"

"Not about the submarines themselves. I was afraid to go too far. Gordon might have become suspicious."

"It's a wonder he didn't. You gathered an amazing amount of information. Why was he so talkative tonight?"

"Male ego." Her smile seemed frozen. "I let him believe he makes me happier than anyone else. That put him in a bragging mood and got him talking about his ship. He sees the *Dolphin*, and its torpedoes, as an extension of his own masculinity."

"Very clever," Hahn said shrewdly. "What better phallic symbol than a torpedo. You're quite perceptive, my dear."

"Not really, Papa. You taught me that man's ego is a fragile thing. I simply play on it and pretend to be a good listener. Almost all of them love the sound of their own voices."

"Particularly when they have a lovely young woman for an audience."

Hahn fell silent, deliberating for a moment. He removed his glasses and massaged the bridge of his nose.

"Let us take stock. You are now involved with officers from the *Dolphin*, the *Sacramento*, the *Arizona*, and the *Enterprise*. Is that correct?"

"Yes."

"Hmmm." He ticked off the count on his fingers. "A submarine, a cruiser, a battleship and an aircraft carrier. Hardly a cross section of so large a fleet. I think we need to broaden the scope of your activities."

"How do you mean?"

"Our orders are to supply the Japanese with critical intelligence. We've not done so to my satisfaction, not yet. I want you to cultivate the company of an officer on the *Lexington*. We need contacts on both carriers."

A shadow seemed to drop over her eyes. "Very well."

"I believe a contact on another battleship would also prove beneficial. Perhaps this Bendix fellow would be suitable."

Her chin tilted. "Do you want me to sleep with him, Papa?"

"Are you asking directions or being impertinent?"

"Why, directions, of course."

"Then let him believe he has seduced you. Play on the male ego you mentioned earlier."

"Seduce the seducer and extract information. Is that it, Papa?"

"Precisely."

"So that would make six."

"Six what?"

"Six men," she said dully. "With whom I sleep regularly."

"I think you are being impertinent."

"No, Papa. It was merely an observation."

Hahn looked at her critically. "What does the number of men have to do with anything?"

"Nothing at all." There was something close to mockery in her voice. "Six or sixty, the number is irrelevant. It is my patriotic duty."

"Consider yourself honored!" Hahn said sharply. "Not many women have such an opportunity to serve the Fatherland."

She managed a strained smile. "Quite true, Papa. I must remember that our boys on the Russian front sacrifice their lives. I give only my body."

She was drained of emotion. Yet it was all she could do to keep the tears from her eyes. She got to her feet and walked toward the door. His voice stopped her.

"You have not been dismissed!"

"What more do you wish, Papa?"

"I want to know your plans for tomorrow."

"Today, Papa. It's already Sunday."

"Very well, today."

"I have a date with Glenn Lockhart. The fighter pilot from the *Enterprise*."

"See to it that you treat him well. I want detailed information — specifics!"

"Why, I thought you knew, Papa. I treat them all well."

She went out. Her mouth was set in an odd smile and a single tear rolled down her cheek. She slowly mounted the stairs.

4

THE HOUR WAS late. Hahn sat alone in the study. His leather bound journal lay open before him on the desk. His expression was analytical as he studied the information, and slowly underlined certain items. Susan's evening had produced an interesting update on the Balao subs. Hahn's eyes were bloodshot and he ached for a decent night's sleep. Yet there was no thought of stopping until he'd completed his report. He was a demanding taskmaster, intolerant of weakness in others. He expected no less of himself.

Greta entered the study. She still wore the gray dress she'd had on earlier that evening. It was one of many plain and colorless frocks that hung in her closet. Hahn willingly splurged on a couturier wardrobe for Susan. He thought of it as an investment, one that paid dividends in the form of attracting naval officers to his daughter. He could think of no good reason to make a similar investment in his wife.

Without a word, Greta sat down opposite him. She crossed her legs and placed a ruled tablet on her knee. Then she uncapped a fountain pen with an unusually fine point. The stroke it produced was wire-thin, allowing great quantities of information to be entered on a single page. She looked up, the pen poised.

Hahn adjusted the glasses. He hunched over the journal, tracing the underlined items with his fingertip. He began dictating.

"Pacific Fleet, Pearl Harbor naval base. Paragraph one. Submarine strength currently unchanged. All ships now equipped with surface radar and must be considered . . . "

The report was concise but detailed. Hahn dictated in a form of verbal shorthand. He stressed the intelligence Susan gathered over the weekend, concluding with a paragraph covering his own activities. Listed were items on the army divisions stationed at Schofield Barracks, as well as various aircraft installations scattered around the island. When he finished, the report was a status summary of the Hawaiian military command. He closed the journal.

"I believe that will suffice."

Greta smiled. "Would I be wrong in saying it's your finest report to date?"

"On the contrary, you're quite correct. Our friend at the consulate will be delighted."

"You must be proud of Susan. She performed exceptionally well this week."

"We must do even better in the future. I'm not yet satisfied with anyone's performance, my own included."

Greta took a deep breath. "May I speak frankly with you, Eric?"

"Of course." Hahn removed his glasses. "What's on your mind?"

"Susan."

"What about her?"

"I think perhaps you ask too much of her."

"I ask nothing of her that I do not demand of myself."

"Forgive me, Eric, but that isn't true."

Hahn scowled. "Are you disputing my word?"

"No," Greta said in a small voice. "I'm attempting to make a distinction. You are not required to . . . prostitute yourself."

"So that's it! You were listening just now."

"Aren't five men enough, Eric? Must you insist that she—"

"Yes, I must insist!" Hahn's face was hard, implacable. "We

each contribute according to our abilities. Her principal ability happens to be in seducing men."

"But she's only a girl. Surely you must realize what it does to her emotionally. If not as a father, then as a psychiatrist. Think what it does to her sense of worth, her self-esteem."

"Her self-esteem? Good God, woman! She should be proud of herself. She serves in the cause of our country. Our Führer!"

"She serves your cause, Eric. You are the one who sought favor with the Führer. Not Susan."

"No more!" Hahn ordered. "I will not be lectured in my own home. The subject is closed."

"Very well," Greta said, her eyes cast downward. "I only wanted you to know I'm terribly concerned."

"Your concern has been noted. Now, let us proceed with tonight's work. Please encode the report."

Dutifully, Greta rose, walked to the bookcase, and selected a Bible, the King James Version. Returning to her chair, she quickly multiplied the date by the month, subtracted from that total the last two digits of the year, then flipped to the corresponding page in the Bible.

She next enciphered the plaintext of the report into codetext. The individual letters of each word were reconstructed in the form of a two-digit number. The first digit represented a line on the page and the second digit represented a letter in that line. She began transposing the coded message onto a single, fresh sheet of typing paper.

Hahn leaned back in his chair. He put his hands behind his head, watching the delicate stroke of her pen. Still angered, he silently considered Greta's accusation. She thought him ruthless and manipulative, driven by some all-absorbing egomania. In private moments, he confessed a certain guilt about the way he'd used their daughter. Yet, from an analytical standpoint, he saw nothing sinister in his motives.

Nor was there any place for bourgeois morality in his work. The conflict, which he'd reconciled in his own mind, stemmed in no way from personal ambition. He was indeed a father, and Susan's well-being mattered very much. But he was first and foremost a German. It was their duty to sacrifice themselves for the glory of the Third Reich and their mission in Hawaii.

After a moment, still preoccupied with thoughts of their assignment, his eyes drifted aimlessly to the open Bible. He recalled how he'd been introduced to the book code. And why. A bright, sunny afternoon in Berlin. A summons to report to Dr. Joseph Goebbels, the Führer's minister of propaganda, and one of the most powerful men in Germany. It was a day Hahn would never forget.

An aide ushered Dr. Hahn into the Reich minister's office. Goebbels greeted him warmly, scrupulously polite. Hahn seated himself, wondering why his daughter's lover would request a meeting. The conversation quickly took a strange turn.

"Earlier today," Goebbels said in a carefully modulated voice, "I spoke with Reichsführer Himmler. He informs me that you are aware of our negotiations with Japan."

"Only the general details. I understand the Führer desires an alliance with Japan."

"Quite so," Goebbels affirmed. "A tripartite alliance uniting Japan, Italy, and Germany. A coalition of the Axis powers."

"Another masterstroke in the Führer's grand design!"

"Very well put, Dr. Hahn. Of course, you realize that such negotiations are delicate, often involving concessions. The Japanese have requested our assistance in a certain matter."

"Indeed?"

"You are, no doubt, familiar with the American naval installation at Pearl Harbor."

"Of course."

"The Japanese wish to establish an intelligence source in Honolulu. Obviously, an Oriental would never be able to infiltrate the American military. We have been asked to provide them with a secret agent."

"A secret agent," Hahn repeated, intrigued by the thought.

"I have discussed the matter with Reichsführer Himmler. We feel you are the very man for the assignment."

Hahn looked surprised. "May I ask why?"

"Several reasons," Goebbels said with a judicial gaze. "You are a man of honor and a loyal party member. We trust you implicitly."

"Thank you, Herr Reich Minister."

"Further, you speak excellent English and you are a family man. An emigre with a wife and daughter would never arouse suspicion."

"Emigre," Hahn said doubtfully. "A political exile?"

"We have devised the perfect cover story. Assuming, of course, that you have no objection to posing as a Jew. Let me explain."

Hahn listened like an assassin at an anatomy lecture. The audacity of the scheme left him fascinated. He saw it as an intellectual challenge, the ultimate cerebral test. Only one thing puzzled him.

"Do I understand correctly? Are you saying my family would be active participants?"

"By all means," Goebbels said in a matter-of-fact tone. "No one would suspect a gracious matron and a beautiful young girl of being spies. The Japanese consider it sheer genius. They approved the idea without a moment's hesitation."

"But my family has no experience in such matters."

"I also spoke with the head of Abwehr One today. That's the department responsible for foreign espionage. You and your family will be trained for intelligence gathering and codes, everything you need. Nothing will be overlooked."

"Pardon my asking," Hahn said slowly. "But does Susan have anything to do with my selection for this assignment?"

"Susan? I fail to see your point, Dr. Hahn."

"By all accounts, you and my daughter are having problems. Perhaps Pearl Harbor represents a discreet solution."

"I beg your pardon!"

"No offense, Herr Reich Minister. But, after all, Hawaii is halfway around the world. It would be the ideal place to exile a troublesome . . . mistress."

"I never allow personal affairs to intrude on affairs of state. To be quite candid, I did recommend you and your family. But only because you are so uniquely suited for the mission. Besides, the Führer himself made the final selection."

"Are you serious? The Führer *personally* chose me?"

Goebbels made an expansive gesture. "I presumed you understood. The Pearl Harbor mission will have a direct effect on our negotiations with Japan. We must succeed, and that makes it imperative that we send only our finest candidate. The Führer believes you to be that man, Dr. Hahn."

Hahn appeared somehow electrified. His eyes were bright and burning. He sat taller in his chair, the look of a zealot etched on his features. He nodded his head formally.

"I serve at the Führer's command."

"Excellent." Goebbels got to his feet. "Please report to Abwehr One tomorrow morning. Your training schedule will be outlined then."

"A question, Herr Reich Minister."

"Yes."

"To whom will I report in Hawaii?"

"Takeo Morimura, the Japanese deputy consul."

Greta's voice broke his spell. He blinked and stared across the desk at her. She held out the sheet of typing paper. It now resembled some ancient parchment covered with hieroglyphics. From top to bottom, it was filled with groupings of two-digit numbers.

"I've finished, Eric."

Hahn took the paper from her. He studied her precise penmanship and marked again that the code was unbreakable. Simply knowing that it was a book code based on the Bible was of no value. Without the key to the page number, there was no way to decipher the message itself.

Hahn folded the paper and placed it inside his journal. Then he opened the center drawer on the desk and tripped a hidden lever. A compartment, cleverly built into the inner well of the desk, popped open. He put the journal in the compartment and closed it. Upon closing the center drawer, the lever snapped into its original position. He stood and stretched.

"Come, my dear. I believe we could both use some sleep. We must be alert tomorrow."

"Yes, Eric."

Greta turned out the light and followed him upstairs.

Hahn stood on the patio. Far below, Pearl Harbor Road was jammed with morning traffic. He raised a pair of naval binoculars and slowly inspected the fleet. There was no change of any consequence, nothing that would materially alter his report. He went back inside.

The house was pleasantly quiet. Susan, as usual, slept late. When Hahn entered the study, Greta was waiting. A copy of the morning *Honolulu Advertiser* was opened on the desk. He retrieved the report from the secret compartment and inserted it behind the front page. Folding the newspaper, he handed it to Greta. Then he checked his watch.

"Take your time," he cautioned. "You can make it easily by eleven. Choose some indirect route."

"I always do."

"Only a reminder, my dear. We can't afford to be careless."

"You needn't worry, Eric. I will remember."

Greta drove from Halawa Heights to downtown Honolulu. She went through the business district and on past the Masonic Temple. Then she turned toward the ocean, winding through the Waikiki beachfront. She arrived at the city zoo shortly before eleven. There she left the car and followed a tree-lined path to Kapiolani Park. Beneath a leafy banyan bower, she took a seat on a shaded bench. She began reading the newspaper.

On the stroke of eleven, she folded the paper and placed it on the bench. She walked away as a slightly-built man appeared from the direction of the beach. He wore a nondescript business suit and his features marked him as Japanese. He strolled to the bench and casually sat down. Several moments elapsed before he picked up the newspaper. He scanned the headlines with mild curiosity. Then he tucked the paper under his arm and got to his feet. He took another path out of the park.

5

SUSAN KEPT BENDIX waiting fifteen minutes. When he had phoned last Sunday, Susan, remembering Hahn's orders, accepted his invitation for dinner the following Saturday.

Entering the living room, she found him talking with her parents. He wore dress whites and his features were tanned from a week at sea. She thought he looked rather dashing, almost debonair. She also thought that he shared her view. He appeared quite impressed with himself.

She was amused by his reaction to her outfit. Whatever he'd expected, she looked considerably different from the night when they had first met. Her velveteen evening skirt was complimented by a faille bodice and a long sleeved bolero jacket. Her hair was upswept, with a string of pearls woven through the braids on top. The only other jewelry she wore were pearl earrings and a stunning diamond solitaire.

The ensemble was a dramatic departure from the halter top she'd worn a week ago. Tonight she looked very much the sophisticate, quite worldly. Bendix was pleasantly surprised, and he clearly approved. His eyes scarcely strayed from her as he bid the Hahns goodnight.

Outside, a flashy Chevrolet convertible stood in the driveway. The car was azure blue with spoked hub caps, and the top was down. Susan thought it somehow matched the man. A convertible was perfectly suited to his image of the dashing young playboy. She idly wondered if he'd had it shipped from the mainland.

Still, she had to admit that it was an evening made for a convertible. The weather was warm and a pale moon hung framed against the starlit sky. From Halawa Heights, the leeward side of the island seemed bathed in a spectral light. The polished hood of the Chevy glimmered as they drove away.

To her surprise, Bendix bypassed the entrance to Pearl Harbor. They drove instead to the Royal Hawaiian Hotel. A landmark of sorts, the Royal Hawaiian catered to Honolulu's social elite. The dining room overlooked the ocean and there was an orchestra every night of the week. The decor was opulent, the service impeccable, and the prices exorbitant. No one was admitted without reservations.

The maitre d' beamed effusively. "Good evening, Commander Bendix."

"Good evening, Jason. Were you able to arrange a nice table?"

"Oh, yessir! No problem at all."

Their table looked out onto the ocean. The crystal stemware gleamed beneath soft candlelight and the linen was immaculate. The maitre d' seated Susan, then imperiously summoned their waiter. An ice bucket appeared, as if by magic, and the waiter popped the cork. After filling their glasses, he bowed and withdrew. Bendix toasted her with a wide grin.

"Here's looking at you, gorgeous."

Susan sipped, watching him with a smile. "Aren't you the clever one? The best table in the house, and champagne already on ice. I'm impressed."

"A special occasion calls for special arrangements. Jason was happy to oblige."

"You're awfully well-known for someone so new to Honolulu. How did you manage all this on a Saturday night?"

Bendix laughed. "Any self-respecting maitre d' has a mercenary nature. His friendship is a negotiable item."

"Then you must be independently wealthy. The navy certainly doesn't pay this well."

"I'm a gambler on the side."

"A gambler?"

"Nothing disreputable," Bendix assured her. "I play the commodities market."

"Do you really! Is that anything like the stock market?"

"It's similar, in the sense that an investor hopes to turn a profit. But the action is considerably faster."

"And you're attracted to fast action?"

Bendix wondered if any double entendre was intended. A shipmate had informed him that his companion tonight was rumored to be a fast lady. But some inner voice warned him that a suggestive reply would be rebuffed. He decided to treat her question in a straightforward manner.

"Anyone who plays commodities has to like fast action. Sometimes you buy and sell on the hour, or quicker."

"Isn't that a bit difficult? I mean, after all, you are out to sea a good deal."

"Well, of course, I operate through a broker. Whenever I place a buy order, I also instruct him at what price to sell. I'm willing to lose a little on the chance I'll make a lot."

"It all sounds terribly complicated. What is it you buy and sell, exactly?"

"Wheat, corn, pork bellies. That sort of thing."

"Are you joking? Pork bellies!"

"Don't laugh," Bendix said jovially. "I've done very well in pork bellies."

"You'll have to admit it's somewhat unusual. A gunnery officer with aspirations of becoming an admiral—who deals in pork bellies."

"Not to toot my own horn," Bendix grinned, "but I'm a pretty unusual fellow. Or hadn't you noticed?"

"Why else would I be here, Harry?"

Susan silently congratulated herself. She had put him in a

chatty mood about his favorite topic: Harry Bendix. She marveled again that there was something of the small boy in every man. They all loved to laud their triumphs, however imaginary. She had only to feed his ego and pretend rapt interest. He would then talk forever.

"I'm curious," she went on. "How did someone like you end up at Annapolis?"

"It was a free education," Bendix said truthfully. "I wanted a college degree and my family couldn't afford the tuition. So I wrangled an appointment to the Academy."

"How marvelous! But I'm still confused. You're obviously quite ambitious, and civilian life offers so much more opportunity. Why make a career of the navy?"

"Several reasons. For one thing, I enjoy the service life. For another, I'm a damned good officer. And last but not least, there's that old motto about 'Join the Navy and See the World.' I guess I'm just a nomad at heart."

"And meanwhile," Susan jested, "you're making your fortune in pork bellies."

Bendix laughed out loud. "Pardon the cliché, but it's like having your cake and eating it too. I've got the best of both worlds."

"So I heard."

"Uh-oh! Somebody been telling tales on me?"

"Well—" Susan let him hang a moment. "I gather you knew John Forster at Annapolis."

"Not socially," Bendix remarked. "I entered the year he graduated. Upperclassmen and plebes aren't exactly on a first name basis."

"How strange. From what he told Kathryn, I just assumed you were great friends."

"Okay, let me have it. What did he say?"

Susan smiled. "He said you were a terrible rogue with the ladies. Kathryn was worried you might take advantage of me."

"And how do you feel about that?"

"I think Kathryn worries too much."

Bendix chuckled appreciatively. Her comment seemed promising, and he decided not to push too far too fast. The night was young and they were only on their first bottle of champagne. He signaled the waiter.

For dinner Bendix ordered escargots, turtle soup, hearts of palm salad, swordfish, and bananas flambée for desert. Susan merely listened, vastly amused, while he made a production of choosing each course. Yet, in spite of herself, she was impressed.

There was a certain style about Harry Bendix. He was arrogant and self-centered, clearly involved in a narcissistic love affair with himself. At the same time, he was urbane and witty, with a touch of polish that stopped short of being suave. Susan found it an altogether intriguing combination. He was deeper than he looked.

She quickly discovered that he was full of surprises. Over dinner, Bendix smoothly switched the conversation from himself to Susan and her family. He seemed genuinely interested and proved to be a good listener, interrupting only to ask an occasional question.

Susan went through her obligatory tale. She related a story of persecution, and the family's ultimate flight to Hawaii. She elaborated briefly on how her father had secreted his wealth from Germany to the safe haven of a Swiss bank account. She ended on a happy, if somewhat poignant, note. She and her family were among the lucky ones — they had escaped.

His reaction was not what she'd expected. Bendix displayed sharp anger that the Nazis had hounded her family into exile. Beneath his anger, however, was an underlying thread of compassion. While he made an effort to hide it, she detected he cared deeply about other people. She thought it revealed yet another aspect of his character, one that tempered the outward facade of egotism. She wondered if she had judged him too quickly, too harshly. Confused, she abruptly turned the conversation in his direction. She asked about his week at sea, and got him talking about the duties of a gunnery officer.

After dinner, a second bottle of champagne materialized in the ice bucket. Susan took it as a signal that it was time to end all serious conversation. Bendix quaffed a glass while it was still bubbling and urged her not to fall behind. Then he whisked her onto the dance floor and gave her a lesson in the latest jitterbug steps from the mainland. For the next hour, they alternated between the dance floor and glasses of hastily sipped champagne. Neither of them noticed that they were attracting glances from nearby tables. Nor were they aware of their own laughter.

Presently Bendix suggested a breath of air. They were both warm from dancing, and an ocean breeze sounded inviting. Wide doors opened onto a terrace at the rear of the dining room. Hand in hand, they made their way outside.

The terrace was bathed in pale moonlight. Below, the surf ebbed and swelled, whitecapped combers gently lapping at the beach. A mantle of stars shone down on the ocean, and seaward, the sky seemed a glittering infinity. From inside, the strains of a haunting melody filled the night.

Susan tensed the moment they stepped through the doors. The spell of the evening was somehow broken by the sound of the surf. As if awakening from a trance, she realized that the champagne and candlelight had been but a prelude. She knew what would happen next and she felt her resolve weaken. She wasn't sure she wanted to resist.

Bendix took her in his arms. He kissed her, and for a moment she clung to his hard, muscular frame. His mouth was like fire on her lips, and her pulse quickened with desire. Then, still holding her, he slowly ended the kiss. He raised his head, staring down at her with a bold look. There was smoldering desire in his eyes, and his smile turned to a rakish grin. He nodded back inside.

"I have a room here at the hotel."

"Oh?"

"On the top floor, with a balcony. Has the greatest view you ever saw. I took it for the weekend."

Susan recoiled at the words. He was expecting an easy conquest, and so confident that he'd already engaged a room. She collected herself, immediately reverting to her original plan. To intrigue him, and capture his interest, she had to create the illusion of a challenge. Unlike other women, she would not jump at the chance of a one-night-stand. Neither would she taunt and tease, or risk threatening his ego. She would simply make him work for it.

"I'm flattered," she said with a warm smile. "And very, very tempted. I really am, Harry."

"That sounds vaguely like a 'no'."

"Only if we're talking about tonight."

"Would the answer be different another night?"

She moistened her lips with the tip of her tongue. "Why not ask and find out . . . another night."

Bendix searched her eyes for a moment. Then his mouth cracked in a sudden grin. He put an arm around her waist and turned her toward the door. As they moved across the terrace, he laughed and shook his head. His voice was thick with wonder.

"I won't ask now, but believe it or not, I will ask."

6

FORSTER KEPT HIS promise. Over the weekend he and Kathryn avoided any mention of her father. The upshot was a measurable improvement in his mood. For the first time in a long while, he got through a weekend without a hangover. He felt somehow restored.

On Monday morning he entered CinCPAC headquarters at 0700. His eyes were clear and his step was almost chipper. He went directly to his office, bypassing the communications room. A stack of messages, decoded over the past twenty-four hours, was sitting on his desk. He sent an orderly for coffee and left word that he wasn't to be disturbed. Then he began reading.

An hour or so later he was finished. He dropped the messages into his OUT basket, ready for filing. There was nothing of consequence in what he'd read, and he was thankful for small favors. Routine matters required no action, which meant no direct report to Ordway. He thought perhaps it was his lucky day. Stubbing out his cigarette, he reached for the phone. It rang as his hand touched the receiver. He lifted it off the hook. "Commander Forster."

"Good morning, Commander." He recognized the voice of Admiral Ordway's aide. "The Old Man wants you up here on the double."

"Problems?"

"I never ask. He just said to make it fast."

"I'm on my way."

Forster hung up the phone. He rose with an inward groan and moved around the desk. His expression was one of mild disgust.

It wasn't his lucky day after all.

"You sent for me, Admiral?"

"Have a seat, Forster."

Ordway waited until he'd taken a chair. With a dark frown, he tossed a communique across the desk, then sat back and bit down hard on his cigar.

"Admiral Kimmel hasn't seen that yet. Look it over and tell me what you think. I have to brief him in a few minutes."

Forster picked up the communique. He saw the designation, TOP SECRET, and quickly scanned the message. His eyes widened.

24 NOVEMBER 1941
FROM: CHIEF OF NAVAL OPERATIONS
ACTION: CINCPAC
CHANCES FAVORABLE OUTCOME OF NEGOTIATIONS WITH JAPAN VERY DOUBTFUL. THIS SITUATION COUPLED WITH STATEMENTS OF JAPANESE GOVERNMENT INDICATE IN OUR OPINION THAT A SURPRISE AGGRESSIVE MOVEMENT IN ANY DIRECTION, INCLUDING ATTACK ON PHILIPPINES OR GUAM, IS A POSSIBILITY. UTMOST SECRECY NECESSARY IN ORDER NOT TO COMPLICATE AN ALREADY TENSE SITUATION OR PRECIPITATE JAPANESE ACTION.

"Good for Washington," Forster said with heavy irony. "I think they've finally seen the light."

"Why do you say that?"

"Because the Jap fleet's steaming around too much for ordinary maneuvers. A task force was sighted off Indochina and a carrier group was sighted off Formosa. Now, we have reports that both units are headed back to Japan."

"Where did the reports originate?"

"British Intelligence," Forster replied. "Separate sightings were made over the weekend. I just finished reading the messages a little while ago."

"And what conclusion do you draw?"

"I think the Japs are trying to hoodwink us."

"How so?"

"For one thing, Admiral, they've made themselves very visible. It's almost as though they wanted to be spotted."

"Why?"

"So we'll believe their Combined Fleet is in home waters. But we have no way of verifying that . . . except through radio traffic."

"Have we done so?"

"No, sir." Forster's face was impassive. "We've had no radio intercepts since the morning of the nineteenth."

"Five days!" Ordway said sharply. "No contact at all?"

"None."

"Why haven't you informed me before now?"

"In effect, Admiral, you told me earlier to keep my theories to myself."

Ordway's mouth tightened. "Whether or not the Philippines are in any danger remains to be seen. For the moment, however, it would seem that Washington shares your view."

"Yes, sir, it would."

"So what's your assessment of the situation?"

"I don't believe either of those task forces are in home waters. I'm convinced they're both steaming toward a rendezvous."

"What intelligence do you have to support your estimate?"

"Not much. It's more a gut feeling than anything."

"In other words, another of your hunches."

"Put yourself in their shoes, Admiral. If you intended to attack the Dutch East Indies and the Philippines, how would you keep it a secret?"

"Evasive action," Ordway said sourly. "And radio silence."

"Which is exactly what the Nips have done."

Ordway dismissed him and hurried off to Admiral Kimmel's office. Walking down the hall, Forster wondered if he would receive credit for the estimate. Then, in the same instant, he laughed softly to himself.

He seriously doubted his name would be mentioned.

7

TAKEO MORIMURA FINISHED knotting his tie. Dinner was served precisely at eight, and he made it a practice to be downstairs early. He saw by the bedstand clock that he had almost a half hour to spare. From his room, he proceeded to the main floor of the consulate. He had developed a fondness for certain Western customs, particularly the cocktail hour. Then, too, a pitcher of very dry martinis made dinner somewhat more bearable. He considered the consul general to be a man of limited intellect. Their conversations were usually quite banal, and inevitably awkward.

A radio clerk intercepted him in the central foyer. The man extended a message form, received only moments ago in the communications room. Morimura saw that it was enciphered in diplomatic code and marked TOP SECRET · URGENT. He noted as well that it was dated November 25, Tokyo time. His before dinner martini was abruptly forgotten.

Hurrying along the hallway, he walked toward the rear of the building. He entered his office and knelt before a squat floor safe. He twirled the combination knob, then opened the door and removed one of several code books. At his desk he painstakingly deciphered the five-letter groupings on the message form. The communique was long and involved, and took almost ten minutes to unscramble. He finally sat back, staring hard at the plaintext, neatly written in his own handwriting. His eyes were like matched black pearls.

IN EVENT DANGER ARISES OF CUTTING OFF DIPLOMATIC RELATIONS, THE FOLLOWING WARNING WILL BE ADDED TO THE DAILY TOKYO SHORTWAVE NEWS BROADCAST.
(1) IN CASE JAPAN - U.S. RELATIONS IN DANGER: HIGASHI NO KASEAME (EAST WIND RAIN).
(2) JAPAN - U.S.S.R. RELATIONS: KITANOKAZE KUMORI (NORTH WIND CLOUDY).
(3) JAPAN - BRITISH RELATIONS: NISHI NO KAZE HARE (WEST WIND CLEAR).
THE SIGNAL WILL BE GIVEN IN MIDDLE AND AT END AS A WEATHER FORECAST AND WILL BE REPEATED TWICE. THEREAFTER, COMMUNICATE ONLY IN EMERGENCY CODE PA - K2.

Morimura read through the message four times. His excitement mounted with each reading. There was no equivocation in the language and the intent of the communique seemed beyond question. Tokyo anticipated not just a breakdown in the negotiations. Instead, there was every expectation that diplomatic relations would be severed completely. And that, in a word, meant war.

Folding the plaintext, he tucked it into his jacket pocket. He then placed the original communique, along with the code book, in the safe. After locking the door, he went outside by way of a rear entrance. He descended a short flight of stairs and walked off in the darkness. The consulate grounds were bordered by a stone wall, with the main gate on Nuuanu Avenue. A few blocks south the lights of downtown Honolulu were visible.

Morimura stopped near the gate. His gaze was drawn eastward to the Punchbowl. High above the center of the city, the rim of the volcanic cone loomed against a starry sky. The sight somehow reminded him of Mount Fujiyama, though it was far less grand in scale. He often stood there thinking of home, wondering if he would ever again see Japan. His thoughts tonight, however, were unencumbered by nostalgia. He contemplated war.

Morimura believed that the Emperor's forces *must* strike, and soon. Japan would exhaust its stockpiles of oil and other war materials within a year, perhaps slightly longer. So the time to strike the British and Dutch was before those stockpiles were depleted. The Japanese Army, with ninety divisions already trained and mobilized, could overrun Asia in a matter of months. The Imperial Navy, meanwhile, could neutralize the Pacific Fleet. Thus would the way be opened for conquest of the Pacific and Australia.

Yet, in Morimura's view, the burden of conquest rested largely on his own shoulders. Expansion of the war in Asia required that the Pacific Fleet be neutralized for at least a year. An invasion of the Philippines, or an aggressive move in the Southern Pacific, required that the Pacific Fleet be all but annihilated. Either of those options was predicated on a surprise attack, with the American warships bottled up in Pearl Harbor. Failing that, Japan dared not advance in any direction.

No one had told Morimura these things. Nor was he privvy to the war plans of the Imperial General Staff. But his meeting with Commander Suzuki had erased any vestige of doubt. Earlier in November, he had met secretly with the staff officer, who was traveling incognito aboard a passenger liner. After the ship departed Honolulu, he'd been certain that a surprise raid on Pearl Harbor was under preparation. There could be no other reason behind Suzuki's request for aerial photographs, and twice-weekly reports on the disposition of the Pacific fleet.

Tonight, the assignment seemed to Morimura an onerous responsibility. His dependence on the Hahns was underscored by their shoddy performance over the past few weeks. Eric Hahn had still failed to produce the aerial photographs. But he was hesitant to reprimand Hahn, or resort to threats. The German was easily offended, and he could hardly afford to alienate his one source of intelligence. Any report, however inadequate, was better than no report at all.

Still, there was no ignoring the passage of time. It had been three weeks since he'd asked Hahn to get aerial photographs and provide twice-weekly reports. The communique in Morimura's pocket placed him under an even greater strain. For he saw now that he was about to be overtaken by events beyond his control. War was imminent, perhaps only a matter of weeks away. And he hadn't a moment to lose.

He turned and walked quickly toward the consulate.

Consul General Nagao Kita was by nature a cautious man. He was small, wore spectacles, and had the cultivated manner of a career diplomat. His composure was monumental. After reading the communique, he took a moment to organize his thoughts. He was annoyed that Morimura had brought it to his attention before dinner, thereby spoiling his appetite. He was also determined not to let his irritation show.

"Well, well," he said with perfect civility. "What do you make of it, Takeo?"

Morimura stared across the desk. They were seated in the consul's office, and no one could hear their words. He saw no reason not to speak his mind.

"I believe it means war."

"Do you?" Kita inquired. "With whom?"

"I beg your pardon."

"Consider a moment," Kita said, a slight fixed smile on his mouth. "Tokyo offers us several alternatives. Among them, the Americans, the Russians, and the British. Which one would you choose?"

Morimura frowned. "Are you serious?"

"Humor me. If you were forced to choose, which would it be?"

"Certainly not the Russians. Not with Hitler's armies at the very gates of Moscow."

"Well, then, that narrows it considerably. We are left with the United States and Great Britain."

"No," Morimyra disagreed. "For *Dai Nippon*, they are one and the same. We cannot attack one without attacking the other."

"In that event," Kita said almost conversationally, "the Emperor's forces would attack Singapore, Java and the Philippines. Is that correct?"

"With one addition. I still believe the Imperial General Staff plans an attack on Pearl Harbor."

"Oh, yes, of course." Kita smiled tolerantly. "Your Pearl Harbor theory. How could I have forgotten?"

Morimura flushed at the patronizing tone. He was only too aware that his presence in the consulate was deeply resented. Kita believed that diplomacy and spying were wholly incompatible. His contempt for those who dealt in espionage was thinly disguised. He made it known by offhand remarks, and a condescending air.

"Perhaps you choose to forget." Morimura looked at him steadily. "But I would remind you that Admiral Nagumo commands a carrier task force. And my orders come direct from him."

"And I would remind you that he takes orders from Admiral Yamamoto. Fortunately, for Japan, Yamamoto is a man of reason and foresight."

"What do you mean?"

"Quite simply, I am saying Admiral Yamamoto would never countenance an attack on the United States. He knows such a war would bring Japan only disaster, and defeat."

"There are those who would call such talk treasonous."

"Treason!" Kita laughed. "Come now, Takeo. Would you care to repeat that accusation to your superiors?"

Morimura was thoughtful a moment. He was accountable only to the Imperial General Staff for his actions. Yet, by virtue of his orders, he was obliged to keep Kita informed. His superiors expected a spirit of "harmony" to prevail, and thus far Kita had proved to be a reasonable man. A personality clash, he told himself now, would reflect badly on everyone concerned. He decided to let it pass.

"It was an observation, not an accusation."

Kita looked at him shrewdly. "Very well, on to other things. What is it you wish of me tonight?"

"Nothing," Morimura replied. "I thought it only courteous to inform you of my plans."

"Are you contemplating anything . . . dangerous?"

"War calls for extraordinary measures. I will do what I must to complete my mission."

"I presume you refer to Dr. Hahn."

Morimura nodded. "I intend to accelerate his activities."

"How will you accomplish that?"

"As you know, his wife acts as our courier. I will forward a message through her."

"I meant," Kita said in a precise voice, "what extraordinary measures will you request of Dr. Hahn?"

"Caution must sometimes give way to audacity. I believe that time has arrived."

"As you say, you do what you must. However, I advise you to do nothing that will jeopardize the negotiations in Washington."

"Surely you don't believe that nonsense in the papers about a compromise. General Tojo would never compromise!"

"We have had no official confirmation to that effect."

"What do you think tonight's communique represents? We have been placed on standby alert."

"Ah, my dear Takeo. You are an innocent when it comes to diplomacy. The negotiations will continue on and on, indefinitely. The longer we talk, the more secure our position becomes on the Asian mainland. You may take my word for it."

"I suggest you read the communique more closely. The language implies that our ambassador has presented not a compromise, but demands. What will happen if America rejects those demands?"

"I doubt very much that our proposal was worded as a demand. Be that as it may, the Americans will merely offer a counterproposal. They do not want a war either."

Morimura's voice was clipped, incisive. "You are right, Consul

General. I have much to learn about diplomacy. But you have a great deal more to learn about men."

"Have I indeed?"

"Yes," Morimura said darkly. "Roosevelt and Tojo both want war. Study their acts, not their words. You will see for yourself."

"How very profound," Kita said with a droll smile. "I had no idea you were a student of human nature."

"Unlike you, Consul General, I am a realist. I accept what is and what will be."

Morimura got to his feet. He nodded his head in a perfunctory bow and walked from the room. Kita was still a moment, then he picked up the communique. He read it through again with closer scrutiny. His eyes narrowed, and his mouth pursed in a thoughtful frown. He grudgingly admitted that Morimura had a point. Words were for diplomats and peacemakers. Warlords spoke through action.

8

SUSAN BROKE HER own rule. She made it a practice never to date the same man two nights in a row. Her seemingly fickle nature somehow made her all the more desirable. Men, like small boys, coveted most what they were regularly denied.

Harry Bendix was the first exception. Last night he'd driven her straight home. He hadn't attempted to paw her or prolong their goodnight embrace. Instead, he kissed her gently, almost tenderly, with great feeling. Then, after inquiring if she'd already made plans for the next night, he very quietly asked her to break the date. She was astonished to hear herself agree.

Later, lying in bed, she wondered at her hasty and curiously impulsive response. She excused it by telling herself that he was a new and important source of intelligence. She reasoned that it was therefore necessary to cultivate him further, enmesh him thoroughly in her web. But she knew, even as she argued with herself, that it was all a shallow pretext. The truth was simpler, admitting to no logic or spidery calculation. He had touched some deep and vulnerable spot within her. A weakness which undermined both resolve and the self-protective veneer of cynicism. Her need to be needed.

Yet she was not comfortable with what she'd done. She awoke disquieted, her perspective altered by daylight. She reminded herself that Bendix, like the other men she dated, was an assignment. The nature of her work made no allowance for emotional involvement. Her father's reaction merely heightened her sense of unease.

After a late breakfast, he had debriefed her in the study. He voiced sharp displeasure that she'd thus far learned nothing of value from Bendix. Her excuses, while credible, did little to allay his anger. She avoided him the remainder of the day, keeping to her room. She was troubled and filled with uncertainty, nagged by a recurring thought. The prospect of seeing Bendix excited her, somehow made her happy, and that was frightening.

Bendix called for her at seven. While they hadn't made specific plans, he had suggested an informal evening. She wore a cotton sundress with patterned lace inset at the bodice and tie straps over the shoulders. Her hair hung loose, and she carried a brightly colored scarf. She looked vibrant, and greeted him with a warm smile. All her worries seemed to dissolve the moment they walked from the house.

Tonight she wasn't surprised when he bypassed the entrance to Pearl Harbor. She got the impression they were going to spend an intimate evening alone. On the way into Honolulu, he patted the seat and grinned. She scooted over beside him, one hand resting lightly on his arm. He glanced at her out of the corner of his eye.

"How does seafood sound?"

"Perfect."

"A buddy told me about a great place on the windward side. He said it overlooks Kaneohe Bay. Good food and a terrific view."

"Oh."

"Anything wrong?"

"No. Why do you ask?"

"Your voice. You don't sound too thrilled with the idea."

"Don't be silly. I love seafood."

"Sure you don't mind the drive?"

"Positive."

She hugged his arm and smiled. But beneath the smile she felt a sharp stab of disappointment. After last night, she'd thought him different than other men. He seemed content not to press her, willing to wait for the right moment. Now, her illusions shattered, she saw that it was merely wishful thinking on her part. He was taking her to the windward side, away from the crowds and the prying eyes of the Officers' Club. Where all the men took their girls for a one-night stand.

Bendix chatted amiably as he drove. He went through downtown Honolulu and turned onto Pali Road. Ahead lay the lofty, fluted spires of the Koolau Range. Soaring skyward, the mountains sheltered the leeward side of the island and turned Waikiki into a sunbather's paradise. The verdant slopes were cloaked in oncoming dusk.

Climbing steadily, Bendix hooked into low gear near the summit. Then the road leveled off and they topped Pali Pass. The gateway to the windward side, the pass burst open onto a spectacular vista of the rugged coastline. Gusty winds whipped through the cut in the mountains, and directly ahead the winding road dropped off sharply. A mantle of darkness abruptly settled over the land.

On the coast Bendix turned westward. The road curved around Kaneohe Bay and a short drive brought them to Kahaluu Point. There, on a finger of land jutting seaward, the lights of a small inn glowed brightly against the shoreline. Not unlike similar establishments on the windward side, it offered food and drink, and a night's lodging. The prices were reasonable, the accommodations were pleasant, and the guests seldom used their real names. The innkeeper was a paragon of discretion.

The atmosphere inside was vaguely oriental. From the lobby Susan and Bendix were led down a narrow hallway. On either side were cozy individual dining rooms screened by sliding doors. They saw no one, since all the doors were closed, and no one saw them. Their room was lighted by scented candles, with a bank of cushy pillows arranged before a low table. The wall opposite the door was a solid pane of glass. It looked out onto the bay, and beyond the breakwater, to the dark swells of the ocean. Visible in the distance was the beam of a mariner's light on Pyramid Rock.

Susan's immediate reaction was one of amusement. It was intimate and romantic, the perfect setting for a seduction. Still, even though it looked somehow staged, she found herself impressed. The view was magnificent, and the privacy was absolute, which was a pleasant change from other inns she'd seen on the windward side. If a girl were to be seduced, she thought, there was something to be said for doing it with style. She idly wondered when Bendix would make his move.

Dinner was a leisurely affair. They were served by a young girl who wore a flowing muumuu and a fresh orchid in her hair. She slipped in and out of the room like a wraith, her passage marked by the faint rustle of the sliding door. She brought them rum drinks with their first course, which was a mixed platter of prawns, squid, and morsels of shark, all cooked over an open brazier. Then she served three piping hot fish dishes, each prepared in savory sauce and surrounded by steamy vegetables. A delicate rice wine, sipped from porcelain cups, complimented the meal.

When they were finished, the girl appeared as though on cue and silently cleared the table. She returned shortly with two snifters and a bottle of Napoleon brandy. Apparently the brandy was the innkeeper's one concession to American tastes. She poured, then placed the bottle on the table and slowly backed to the door. She looked them full in the eyes for the first time and smiled like an elfin conspirator. Her voice was a melodic, singsong chant as she slipped through the door.

"Goodnight, pleasant dreams. You will not be disturbed further. Goodnight."

Susan suppressed a laugh. Throughout dinner Bendix had entertained her with anecdotes from his days at Annapolis. His mood was carefree and relaxed, and there was nothing in his manner to suggest a sexual overture. But now, she thought the situation was all too obvious. They were alone, surfeited with food and wine, and the serving girl had all but tucked them in for the night. She sipped her brandy in silence, waiting for his opening line. She expected something glib and clever.

Bendix eased back on the fluffy pillows. He smiled, watching her a moment, then his eyes shifted to the window. Far out to sea a tongue of lightning streaked the sky. The darkness was split with an instant of dazzling white clarity, illuminating the horizon. He shook his head with mild wonder.

"Looks like a storm's brewing."

"Oh?"

"If I'm any judge—," He paused, another bolt of lightning reflected in his eyes. "We'll get hit with a rain squall in an hour, maybe less."

"You sound concerned. Will it be that bad?"

"Only if you don't mind getting wet. The top doesn't work on my car. I keep forgetting to have it fixed."

"Usually rain squalls pass fairly quickly."

Bendix nodded toward the window. "We won't outrun that one. It'll catch us just about the time we cross the mountains."

Her voice was puzzled. "Are we leaving?"

A beat of silence slipped past. "Why not?" Bendix asked. "Unless you tell me you prefer to stay."

There it was, the invitation. But stated in a way she'd never anticipated. He had arranged the dinner, purposely created the time, the place and the opportunity. Yet now, true to his promise, he was making no demands. She recalled the way he'd said it last night. *I won't make a move till you give me the word.*

So it was up to her. She realized that he would say nothing more. Nor would he touch her or attempt to take advantage of the situation. He would, instead, abide by whatever she decided. Her heart pounded and her throat went dry. She suddenly comprehended that he was no longer an assignment. He was a man who wanted her and needed her. And she needed him.

"Last night—," Her voice was barely audible. "You left it up to me to say the word."

"Are you saying it now?"

She nodded almost imperceptibly. "I believe the word is . . . yes."

Susan was always to remember that moment. His arms enfolded her in an embrace, and her last defenses crumbled. Her mouth opened, moist and inviting, and he kissed her. She felt an unbearable excitement as he untied the straps on her sundress. Her hands cupped his face, caressing the hard line of his jaw, and she trembled. He lowered her onto the pillows and within moments they were naked.

Then his arms went beneath her. She was lifted, pressed closer still. Time lost measure and meaning as she crossed a threshhold far beyond the limits of her most vivid fantasies. Their bodies were joined in perfect union. In that final instant, she clung to him in an exquisite agony of release.

For a long while they were content with the silence, drifting on a quenched flame. Then they kissed again, their bodies warm and their legs entwined. She knew, at last, the difference between sex and making love. When they parted, he tenderly stroked her hair, stared intently into her eyes. He kissed the tip of her nose, almost spoke, then stopped as though searching for words. His voice was hoarse.

"I've never said this before . . ."

"No." She pressed her fingers to his lips. "Don't say it now."

"Why not? Wasn't it the same for you?"

"You shouldn't have to ask."

"Then you know that it was more than . . . physical."

"Yes, I know. I felt it too."

"So why shouldn't I say what I'm feeling . . . what we're both feeling?"

"Please, not now. Not yet."

Her mind was a flux of emotions. She dared not let him speak of love. She dared not allow herself even to think of love. Her father would never permit it, and she dared least of all to defy him. Her body was still his to command, and she could give herself wholly to no man. She could only hope that the one beside her now would somehow understand. And ask no more than she'd given of herself tonight.

"Hold me, Harry. Don't say anything else . . . just hold me."

His voice was husky. "I want you to marry me . . . be my wife."

She tensed, started to pull away. His arms tightened, holding her fast. He went on before she could protest.

"You asked me not to say it, but you'd have to cut my tongue out to stop me. I love you—"

"Please don't."

"—and I want you to marry me. I've never said that before, not to anyone. You're the first, Susan. The very first."

"I can't marry you. I can't!"

He took her face in his hand. Then, tilting her head, he forced her to meet his gaze. "Do you love me?"

"Oh, Harry, please don't. You could have any girl you want. You know you could."

"You're avoiding the question."

"I won't answer you."

"Why not?"

"Why should I?"

"Because I think I deserve an answer, don't you?"

Her eyes were tormented. "Yes."

"Don't lie." He watched her intently, her features distinct in the glow of the candles. "Whatever the truth is, I'll see it in your face. Do you love me?"

"Yes."

Her throat seemed to constrict around the word. Her eyes glistened, and tears suddenly spilled down her cheeks. She buried her head against his chest, sobbing quietly. He held her a moment without speaking, gently stroking her hair. Then he leaned down, kissed away her tears.

"You love me."

"Yes."

"Say it."

"Oh, Harry, stop! Please stop. You knew I loved you without asking."

"Then why can't you marry me?"

Her voice was choked. "Because I . . . do . . . love . . . you."

He stared at her. "That doesn't make sense. You can't marry me because you love me."

"Yes." She averted her eyes. "Please don't ask me to explain. It's just the way things are. Won't you believe me?"

"Not things." His gaze sharpened. "It's your father, isn't it?"

"No! Why do you say that?"

He heard the lie in her voice. Several times before he'd thought his imagination was playing tricks on him. At the Hahn home, when he'd called for her, he had the eerie impression she was frightened of her father. Nothing tangible, nothing overt, but a sensation each time he'd seen them together. Now he knew his instincts hadn't failed him after all. Her look transcended fear or fright. She was terrified.

"Tell you what," he said reassuringly, "I'll speak to your father about it. He doesn't seem all that unreasonable to me."

Her mouth ovaled in a quick intake of breath. She wrenched free of his embrace and somehow collected herself. She swiped away the last tear with the back of her hand.

"Listen to me," she said, her voice strangely calm. "You mustn't say a word to my father. Not now, not ever. That would ruin any chance we might have."

"What chance do we have if I don't?"

"Please, I beg you to understand. If you say anything—anything at all—he will forbid me to see you. You must believe me, Harry."

"I don't get it. You've dated lots of guys and he never objected."

Bendix instantly regretted the words. He knew she was a woman of experience, no virgin. But then, he was hardly a saint himself. What was past was past, and required no explanation. His only concern was the future, their future.

"What I'm trying to say," he went on lamely, "why would your father object to marriage?"

She steeled herself to sound convincing. "In some ways, he's still very old world. He allows me to date, but he would never allow me to marry, not without his blessing. He sees that as a father's right—his duty."

"I'm really confused! You say you can't marry me because you love me. Now you say you need your father's blessing. None of it makes any sense. It's crazy!"

"Trust me." She kissed him lightly on the mouth. "Let me work it out in my own way. Please."

"Does that mean you'll talk to your father?"

"Yes, very soon. When the time seems right. I promise."

"And what am I supposed to do in the meantime?"

"You could start by making love to me again."

She slipped into his arms, found his mouth. She stilled his protests, quickly beguiled him, again bought his trust. And all the while she hated herself.

9

A SINGLE LAMP burned in the living room. Hahn was seated in an armchair, the evening newspaper spread across his lap. His stare was fixed on the middle distance. Since dinner, he hadn't spoken to Greta. He seemed withdrawn and introspective, preoccupied with some weighty problem. She had wisely refrained from bothering him, interrupting only when it was time for bed. He'd scarcely acknowledged her goodnight.

A small Dresden clock on the mantle chimed the half hour. He checked his watch and saw that it was two-thirty. Apparently he'd been sitting there, staring at the wall, for almost two hours. He removed his glasses and slowly massaged his eyes. He felt worn to the bone.

The front door opened, then closed. He placed the newspaper and his glasses on the lamp table. Staring past the light, he peered through the living room door. He saw movement in the darkened foyer.

"Susan?"

"Yes, Papa."

"I would like a word with you."

Susan appeared in the doorway. Her hair was windblown and her dress was creased with wrinkles.

"What is it, Papa?"

"Please be seated."

She went to the sofa and sat down with a feigned look of exhaustion. "Couldn't it wait till morning, Papa? I'm very tired."

"I shouldn't wonder," Hahn said sharply. "You look a mess. Your mother tells me you were out with Bendix again."

"Yes, that's right," she said indifferently.

"Until nearly three in the morning?"

"Well, it isn't all that unusual, Papa. I often stay out late."

"And lately with Bendix."

"Oh, honestly, Papa! You're imagining things."

"I imagine nothing." Hahn's voice was deceptively soft. "Your other gentlemen friends provide reams of intelligence. From Bendix you have obtained only the most superficial information."

She looked at him blankly. "I presume it's because he only recently joined the fleet. What other reason would there be?"

A long moment of appraisal slipped past as Hahn examined her. Then his features took on a hard cast. "Something bothers me about this Bendix. You haven't become attached to him, have you?"

There it was. The question she feared most. Her breath caught in her throat, and she involuntarily blinked. She struggled to maintain her composure.

"Now you are imagining things, Papa. Harry Bendix means nothing to me. Absolutely nothing!"

Hahn's eyes were very pale and direct. "Good. Then you won't mind not seeing him again, will you?"

"Why would I do a thing like that?"

"For the simplest of reasons. I want you to eliminate Bendix from your list of suitors."

"Are you forbidding me to see him?"

"Precisely."

A sudden anger welled up in her. All her life she'd been manipulated by men, most notably her father. Now he was about to destroy the only genuine love she had ever known. The thought of losing Bendix, like tinder to spark, ignited a sort of frenzied desperation. She seemed to draw on some inner reserve of strength, ruthlessly suppressed her fear. She stood erect, facing him.

"I'm afraid I can't do that, Papa."

"May I ask why not?"

"Harry Bendix asked me to marry him tonight."

Hahn appeared incredulous. "And you accepted?"

"I told him I would think about it. You just now made my decision for me."

"Tomorrow morning"—Hahn leveled a finger at her—"you will call Bendix and break off the relationship. You are never again to see him or speak to him!"

"No," she said defiantly. "I love him and I intend to marry him. You can't stop me, Papa."

"I *order* you to do as you are told!"

"And I refuse."

Hahn exploded from his chair. He took a quick stride forward and backhanded her across the mouth. The blow knocked her off her feet and sent her sprawling. Her eyes glazed, and she dropped heavily onto the sofa, her legs akimbo. A trickle of blood seeped down her chin.

"You will obey!" Hahn shouted. "I will tolerate no further insolence. Do you understand?"

She attempted to rise, groggily sat down. Her vision was still blurred. "I'm not a whore, Papa. I have feelings."

"You were Goebbels' whore! Why else do you think you were selected for this mission? You have a whore's mind and a whore's body. You enjoy it!"

She experienced an instant of dawning comprehension. She saw etched on his features all the rage and frustration of an irate father. Suddenly she understood why he'd bartered her like a common streetwalker. He loathed himself for encouraging her relationship with Goebbels, trading on it. So he had expunged his guilt by debasing her, transforming her into something unworthy of love. He sold her to other men.

"Oh, my God!" she cried. "You did it on purpose. You turned me into a whore . . . to save yourself!"

"What?" Hahn stared at her as though he couldn't have heard correctly. "What did you say?"

"I said I'm going to marry Harry Bendix. I'm through being your whore."

"You contemptible little . . ."

Hahn yanked her off the sofa. He grabbed her arms and shook her so hard her head snapped back and forth. The straps of her dress tore loose and his grip tightened into her flesh. He abruptly pulled her so close that their faces almost touched.

"Listen very carefully. Unless you do as you're told, I will contact Morimura. I will inform him that Bendix endangers our operation."

"You wouldn't!"

"Wouldn't I?" Hahn said, his voice cold as ice, "And do you know what Morimura would do? He would kill your precious Bendix without a moment's hesitation."

All the color drained from her face. She felt as though her insides had turned to stone, and her resolve suddenly weakened. A stricken look crossed her features. She shook her head violently. Her words were a hushed whisper.

"I won't see him again, ever. I swear it."

Hahn laughed. It was an odd laugh, harsh and brutal. He released her, airily waved his hand. "I've changed my mind. You will be permitted to see Bendix — let us say . . . once a week."

She looked dazed, bewildered. "Why?"

"Why not?" Hahn gently pinched her cheek. "I want you to be happy, *liebchen*. Enjoy yourself with this Bendix fellow. But no more talk of marriage."

"Do you really mean it, Papa?"

"Of course! We'll just consider your night with Bendix as your day of rest. The other nights of the week you will continue to obey me and perform your *duties*." He laughed, mocking her. "Won't you?"

In utter desolation, she turned and ran blindly up the stairs.

Greta entered her bedroom some minutes later. Susan sat at

the vanity table, her knuckles pressed white against her teeth. Her eyes were vacant.

"Look at me, child." Greta tenderly turned her face to the light. "*Gott in Himmel!* I prayed I was wrong."

"It's nothing, Mama. I'm not hurt."

Susan's bottom lip was split, slightly puffed. Greta hurried to the bathroom and returned with a damp face cloth. She gingerly dabbed away the caked blood, muttering to herself in German. Then she gave Susan the cloth and made her press it lightly to the swollen lip. She sat down on the edge of the bed.

"Why did your father strike you?"

"I received my first marriage proposal tonight, Mama. Harry Bendix asked me to be his wife."

"And you told your father?"

"Yes—"

Susan choked, unable to continue. She squeezed her eyes so tightly shut that tears were forced out beneath the lashes. Her lip trembled, and after a moment she sponged her eyes with the cloth. She found a shred of voice.

"Was I asking so much, Mama? It seems so little, to marry someone you love. He hit me and called me a whore. He threatened to have Harry killed."

"We are German," Greta said heavily. "To your father, that means duty and country before family."

"Japan isn't our country! Haven't we the right to a private life? Doesn't happiness count for something, Mama?"

Greta heard the pain in her voice, slowly nodded. "Once, long ago, I too loved a man. But he was not a man who pleased my father. So a marriage was arranged and I became Frau Hahn." She paused, looked down at her wedding band. "Sometimes our duty permits no love. We do what we must . . . and accept it."

Susan was momentarily speechless. She looked at her mother as though seeing her for the first time. She saw vestiges of the young girl who long ago had loved and lost. A girl very much like herself.

"Why have you never told me before, Mama?"

"I have told no one. Not even your father knows the whole truth. He still believes I came to our wedding bed a virgin."

"Are you saying you were pregnant . . . with me?"

"No, no." Greta reached out, squeezed her hand. "You are your father's daughter. I speak now of my young man only for a reason."

"A reason?"

Greta's voice dropped. "You must learn from me as I learned from my mother. A woman sustains herself in this life on hope. Our hope that we will outwit, or at least outlive, the men in our lives. Without that hope, we are doomed."

"And have you outwitted Papa?"

"Not yet. But I will . . . through you."

"How?"

"Because you will have your love, your young man."

"I will?"

"Yes."

Greta spoke the word with an unyielding sense of finality. She stared at her daughter without expression for a moment. Then the line of her mouth crooked in a severe smile.

"I swear it on your father's head."

10

SUSAN IGNORED THE stares. She'd long since lost interest in the officers and their ladies. Her past efforts to titillate them now seemed to her somehow vulgar. It smacked of low farce.

Her outfit nonetheless turned heads. As she entered on the arm of Glenn Lockhart, the crowd appeared to pause in a moment of collective inspection. She wore an ivory jacquard blouse, v-necked with long sleeves, and an evening skirt of pleated silk. The blouse, cut daringly low, was revealing. She looked at once chic and wanton.

Lockhart enjoyed the attention. His mouth curled in a smirky grin as he led her across the room. She let him have his moment, wholly indifferent to the stares. Her eyes went instead to their table. She saw that it was unoccupied, no sign of Kathryn and Forster. She thought it very unlike them to be late, and wondered why they'd been detained. Then Lockhart held out her chair, still playing to their audience with his grin. She sat down quickly.

While Lockhart ordered drinks, she casually looked around the room. She saw nothing of Bendix, even though his ship had docked late that afternoon. Their next date was set for Sunday night, and she hadn't expected him to call. But she missed him terribly, ached to be with him and hear his voice. At the same time she hoped he would bypass the club tonight, go somewhere else. She didn't want to see him with another woman.

A few day's separation had done nothing to alter her feelings. With an opportunity to think it through, she realized he had shown her the hidden hungers of her emotions. What she felt for him, and what he gave her, transcended the physical. He satisfied her need to be wanted for herself, rather than as a sexual plaything. She was made whole, somehow complete, by the emotional bond. And she knew that everything she felt was exactly the same for him. So it was just as well that he didn't see her with another man.

When their drinks were served, Lockhart offered a jocular toast. "Here's looking at you, doll! Everybody else was when we came through the door."

"I think you're exaggerating, Glenn."

"Not a whole lot. You stopped the conversation cold."

"How inconsiderate of me," Susan said with a disarming smile. "I hope I haven't offended anyone."

"You're safe there. Besides, they needed something different to talk about anyway."

"Different?"

"You know, after the last couple of days."

"I stayed home last night. Has something happened?"

"You haven't heard?"

"No."

"The fleet was put on combat alert."

Susan was instantly attentive. Aircraft carriers, for reasons she'd never fully understood, were ususally the first ships to be alerted during war games or mock drills. As a pilot on the *Enterprise*, Lockhart was a particularly valuable source of information. She forced herself to remain calm.

"Why?" she asked in a normal tone of voice. "What caused the alert?"

"Washington broke off negotiations with the Japs. Not that anybody's saying it out loud. But there's been speculation on all the news reports."

"Oh, it couldn't be all that serious. I think reporters tend to blow things out of proportion."

"Guess again," Lockhart told her. "According to scuttlebutt, there's even a sabotage alert. All the Japs here on Oahu are under suspicion."

"Well, it sounds to me like overreaction on someone's part. Are you sure these aren't just wild rumors?"

"No, it's not rumors. I've seen the extra guard details myself."

"I still have trouble believing it."

Lockhart's reply was cut short. Kathryn and Forster appeared in the doorway, and moved toward the table. Susan waved, noting that Kathryn looked especially attractive tonight. Her hair was upswept in a mass of golden curls, and her fawn-colored evening gown complemented her sunny complexion. She began talking even before she sat down.

"Sorry we're late. John got held up at the last moment. God, Susan, you look ravishing tonight!"

"I've been telling her the same thing," Lockhart beamed.

"Susan." Forster nodded, dropped into his chair. "Evening, Lockhart."

"How are you, Commander?"

"I'll have to admit I've had better days."

"Don't mind him," Kathryn chided. "He has an advanced case of the grumps. I almost came alone."

Forster signaled their waiter. "All I need is a drink. Or maybe a double to start with."

Kathryn rolled her eyes. Susan sensed they'd had words on the way to the club. Forster actually sounded churlish, almost quarrelsome. His mood, added to the fact he'd worked late, indicated that it somehow involved his duties. She wondered if the international situation was as tense as Lockhart would have her believe. She was hesitant to raise the subject too openly.

Lockhart saved her the trouble. He waited until Forster was halfway through a double scotch. Then he leaned forward with a knowing look. "Commander, I was just telling Susan about the latest scuttlebutt. What's your opinion?"

"What scuttlebutt?"

"The combat alert and all this stuff we've heard about sabotage. Any truth to it?"

Forster's voice was abrupt. "You talk too much, Lieutenant."

"John!" Kathryn exclaimed.

Forster silenced her with a look. "It's no time for a loose lip. And you shouldn't have to be told that, Lockhart."

"Oh, really now," Susan said lightly. "Aren't you being a little hard on Glenn? I wouldn't repeat anything he said. Not a word."

"Perhaps not," Forster replied. "But that still doesn't excuse it."

"Well, hell," Lockhart said defensively. "It's not like I'm broadcasting secrets. Nobody's talked about anything else since yesterday."

Forster stared at him. "Then I'd suggest you set the example — starting now."

"Honestly!" Susan laughed. "I think you need more than a double, Commander Forster. Come on, Glenn, let's dance."

Lockhart hastily rose to his feet. He gave Susan a look of deliverance and led her to the dance floor. She stepped into his arms as the orchestra opened a medley with "A-Tisket A-Tasket." They were quickly lost within the crowd.

Forster lapsed into a brooding silence. He was somewhat nonplused by his own behavior. He tried to analyze why he'd come down so hard on Lockhart. Nothing reasonable occurred to him, with one slight exception. Susan Hahn was not "navy." To get technical about it, she wasn't even American. She was, in every sense of the word, an outsider. And her popularity with single officers in no way altered that fact. He subjected the thought to closer examination.

"John."

Kathryn's voice was an intrusion. He scarcely glanced at her. "What is it?"

"I was kidding when I said I almost came alone tonight."

"Yeah, I know."

"I'm not kidding now," Kathryn said coolly. "Either you

straighten up and fly right—or I'll *leave* here alone."

Forster started as though she'd slapped him. "Aren't you playing a little rough?"

"No, you are!" Kathryn countered. "You were out of line and downright rude. You had no right to treat Glenn that way."

"All right, so I was rough on him. There's still no excuse for loose talk."

"Don't be ridiculous! Every sailor on Hotel Street is blabbing the same thing. Do you deny it?"

Forster could only agree. Honolulu's whorehouse district was probably alive with talk of the combat alert. He slowly shook his head.

"Kate, I'm under a lot of pressure. There are things happening that I can't even repeat to you."

"Are you trying to make a point?"

"Pressure sometimes plays funny tricks on the mind. I think I jumped on Lockhart because of Susan."

"Susan!"

Forster shrugged. "She bothers me. Stop and think about all these men she dates. And yet she's supposedly moonstruck on Bendix." He paused, his expression troubled. "Something just doesn't jell."

"For your information"—Kathryn's look was frosty—"I had lunch with Susan yesterday. She explained the whole thing."

Kathryn briefly recounted the luncheon. Forster appeared dumbfounded when she told of Bendix's marriage proposal. He listened without interruption while she outlined the conditions imposed by Susan's father. Yet the brooding look never completely disappeared from his eyes.

"So there!" Kathryn concluded. "Don't you feel the least bit silly now?"

"Maybe so, maybe not. Why doesn't Susan just elope? She's a big girl."

"I am too," Kathryn said pointedly. "And we're still tiptoeing around my father, aren't we?"

"Touché."

Forster averted his gaze. It was all very rational, a reasonable explanation for Susan's behavior. But instinct, that visceral unease, sometimes prevailed over reason. He reminded himself to call the FBI first thing Monday morning. He wanted a rundown on Dr. Eric Hahn.

"Forster sure likes to pull rank. I almost told him to . . ."

"I think you handled it like a perfect gentleman."

"You do?"

Susan smiled sweetly. "Just between us, John's behaving very boorishly tonight. Even Kathryn thinks so."

Lockhart steered an uneven course across the dance floor. His eyes kept shifting back to the table, and Forster. He was simmering with barely contained anger.

"I'll tell you one thing," he muttered. "Forster's full of you know what. He acts like it's a big dark secret!"

"Secret?"

"The war! Everybody knows we're gearing up to fight Japan."

"Are we really?" Susan coaxed. "How can you be so certain?"

"Why do you think I'm sailing tomorrow?"

"Not on a war mission!"

Lockhart swelled with sudden importance. "It's the next best thing. They needed a carrier to ferry a squadron of fighters out to Wake Island. So they just naturally picked the *Enterprise*."

"How exciting." Susan looked at him with open admiration. "But why couldn't the planes just fly there?"

"Too far. Wake's about halfway between here and the Philippines."

"Oh, I see. It's like an outpost."

"Yeah, exactly. Only if you want my opinion, it's a waste of planes. The Nips will hit the Philippines first — and hardest."

Susan frowned. "Will you be gone long?"

"Why do you ask?"

"Well, it all sounds so dangerous. I'll worry about you."

"Worry about those Marine pilots, not me. Our orders are to put them within flying distance of Wake and then head home. I'll be back before you know it."

Lockhard almost stopped dancing. Then he woofed a low, rumbling chuckle. "Yikes! I'm glad Forster can't hear me now. He'd really singe my tail feathers."

"I won't tell if you don't."

"You're my girl, Susie!"

Susan placed her head on his shoulder. For some reason, the nickname no longer offended her. He was, like all the men she dated, simply too naive for his own good. And her deceit, in the face of such trust, suddenly seemed low and vile. A wave of guilt and self-revulsion swept over her.

One feeling led unwittingly to another. John Forster was neither naive nor trusting. She heard again his harsh tone and the cynicism behind his words. Thinking back, it occurred to her that his reprimand was too quick, almost an involuntary reaction. She wondered whether he would have rebuked an officer whose lady was "navy." Or anyone at all except for her presence at the table.

She thought not. And curiously, she didn't question what her intuition told her. She was, instead, afraid.

11

TANKAN BAY WAS some four hundred miles north of Tokyo. A natural anchorage, located in the Kurile Islands, the bay was sheltered by bleak gray mountains. It was the rendezvous point for the Pearl Harbor Striking Force.

Admiral Chuichi Nagumo stood on the bridge of his flagship, the carrier *Akagi*. At anchor around him were five carriers, two battleships, three cruisers and nine destroyers. Auxiliary craft, positioned astern of the warships, included eight oil tankers and four cargo vessels. A pack of twenty-five submarines already preceded the main force by several hours.

Dawn was only minutes away. Fog wreathed the rocky coastline and inland, the desolate mountains were crowned with snow. Admiral Nagumo was alone on the bridge, and as the sky paled in the east, he suddenly felt the burden of leadership. His appointment as commander of the Striking Force made him responsible for the largest naval armada ever assembled by *Dai Nippon*.

The course charted to Hawaii was across the northern route. Admiral Nagumo, over the objections of the Imperial Staff, had personally selected the longer and more arduous approach. Despite prevailing bad weather and high seas, he believed it would reduce the chance of detection by American patrol planes. He understood that the margin for error was zero. His orders were to turn back immediately if sighted.

Preparation for the mission had begun almost a year ago. The object was to destroy the Pacific Fleet and, at first, the prospects of success appeared slight. Hawaii was thousands of miles away, with airfields strategically scattered around the island of Oahu. Worse, Pearl Harbor itself was quite shallow, which created problems for the torpedo planes. Only after extensive experiments were reliable shallow-draft torpedoes developed. Finally, from intelligence gathered by agents in Honolulu, it was determined that an arrow-like lane of water led straight to the battleship moorings on Ford Island. The plan, while still hazardous, at last seemed feasible.

By late August, Admiral Isoroku Yamamoto unveiled the Order of Battle for the Combined Fleet. Pearl Harbor would be attacked on a Sunday, when major elements of the American fleet were in port for the weekend. Simultaneously, an invasion would be mounted on Singapore, with sea and air assault followed by troop landings. Hours later, still another task force would commence operations against the Philippines. A study performed by the Imperial War College indicated the Pearl Harbor Striking Force would lose only two carriers. Staff planners considered it an acceptable loss in exchange for destruction of the Pacific Fleet. The date set for the attack was December 7, Honolulu time.

For Admiral Nagumo, the optimism of Staff planners seemed wildly premature. Everything hinged on the execution of his mission. Unless the Pacific Fleet was annihilated, the invasion of the Philippines, not to mention Singapore, was almost certainly doomed to failure. Yet there were only slightly more than four hundred bombers and fighters aboard his aircraft carriers. Based on intelligence reports, he knew there were almost an equal number of American planes on Oahu. His warships, moreover, were outnumbered roughly three to one. So he had grave reservations about the War College study. Barring absolute and total surprise, he would lose considerably more than two carriers. He might very well lose his entire command.

A footstep sounded behind him. Nagumo turned and saw

Commander Suzuki approaching. The young naval officer had only recently returned to Japan. His voyage aboard the passenger liner, with stops in Honolulu and Los Angeles, had provided vital intelligence data. But now, as the time of departure neared, Nagumo felt the need of reassurance. He had summoned Suzuki to the flagship.

"Good morning, Commander."

"Admiral." Suzuki saluted, stiffly correct. "You sent for me, sir?"

"I wish to review certain matters regarding Pearl Harbor."

"Yes, sir."

"In our previous conversation, you made reference to your contact in Honolulu. What was his name again?"

"Deputy Consul Morimura, sir."

"It occurs to me that I forgot to ask the most salient question. How reliable do you consider Morimura's information?"

Suzuki sensed something unspoken. The admiral's features were set in a stern mask, his eyes intense. He was a small man, slightly built, with graying hair and a soft-spoken manner. But his reputation as an iron disciplinarian was legend throughout the fleet. Suzuki chose his words with care.

"Sir, I believe the information to be correct. Under Morimura's direction is a German agent, and more importantly, the German's daughter. She is our primary source of intelligence on the Pacific Fleet."

"And you trust her implicitly?"

"Yes, Admiral, I do. Her record is without blemish."

Nagumo eyed him keenly. "Are you satisfied that the American warships always return to Pearl Harbor on weekends?"

"It is their custom, Admiral. On weekends, only a token force puts to sea."

"And their aircraft carriers?" Nagumo demanded. "We cannot risk air attack while our own planes are over Pearl Harbor. I believe you see my point."

"Yes, sir. Our reports, however, indicate a definite pattern. At least one, and usually both of their carriers are in port on weekends. And I might add, Americans are very much creatures of habit. They seldom deviate from established practice."

"Let us pray you are right, Commander. We stake the Empire on the word of a German girl. I would prefer something of more substance."

"Yes, sir."

"Thank you. I have no more questions."

After Suzuki withdrew, Admiral Nagumo walked forward. He clasped his hands behind his back and watched dawn slowly emerge from the sea.

On November 30, Admiral H. E. Kimmel called an emergency staff meeting. Attending were Vice Admiral Ordway, the three Battle Force commanders and all CinCPAC section chiefs. Forster stood with the other staff members at the rear of the room.

Just days before, Secretary of State Hull had delivered an ultimatum to the Japanese Ambassador in Washington. The message was in response to the proposal of the Japanese Government. By order of the President, Hull insisted categorically that all troops be withdrawn from China and Indochina. Further, he demanded that the Japanese Government withdraw as a member of the Axis powers. He bluntly refused to negotiate further until Japan evidenced some new measure of good faith.

Today, Admiral Kimmel assembled his staff to hear a communique from the Chief of Naval Operations. He asked Admiral Ordway to read the message aloud, verbatim. Ordway cleared his throat and proceeded in a strong voice.

"THIS DISPATCH IS TO BE CONSIDERED A WAR WARNING. NEGOTIATIONS WITH JAPAN HAVE CEASED. AN AGGRESSIVE MOVE BY JAPAN IS EXPECTED WITHIN THE NEXT FEW DAYS. EXECUTE AN APPROPRIATE DEFENSIVE DEPLOYMENT PREPARATORY TO CARRYING OUT THE TASKS ASSIGNED IN WAR PLAN 46."

Ordway paused, then went on. "Effective immediately, gentlemen, all commands will implement the Joint Army-Navy Hawaiian Defense Plan."

Every officer present was familiar with the particulars. Under the guise of field maneuvers, General Short's infantry would man beach emplacements around the island. All naval units, while in port, would be placed on Condition Three. This was a low-level standby alert under which one-third of the antiaircraft guns were to be manned on each watch. No one seriously expected a land invasion by Japanese troops. Nor was there any great concern of an air attack on Pearl Harbor. The Hawaiian Defense Plan was a paper exercise created to satisfy the War Department.

"Now," Ordway continued, "as to the second part of the dispatch. War Plan 46 provides for several contingencies. Our principal concern, of course, is the Philippines. In the event of hostilities, we would move at all speed to engage the Japanese fleet. However, under no circumstances are we to initiate aggressive action." He paused, glancing at Kimmel. "I believe that covers it, Admiral."

"Thank you, Tom."

Kimmel seemed to gather his thoughts. Then he addressed himself to the assembled officers. "Gentlemen, as you know, the Philippines are in bad shape. The Asiatic Fleet, under Admiral Hart, has only two cruisers and a handful of destroyers. For all practical purposes, they are capable of little more than a holding action."

Hesitating, Kimmel stared at them solemnly. "I believe we can assume the Pacific Fleet will be called upon to reinforce the Philippines. In the meantime, see to it that your commands are in a state of combat readiness. Are there any questions?"

"Admiral." Forster took a step forward. "I have two dispatches that came in just before you called the meeting."

Ordway shot him a look. Kimmel, unaware of the byplay, nodded. "Please be brief, Commander."

Forster unfolded the message forms. "The first is from Naval Intelligence. It advises us to expect subversive activities from the local Japanese population. I presume the word 'subversive' refers to acts of sabotage."

"How many Japanese are there on the islands?"

"No one knows, sir. Not for certain. Civilian authorities estimate a figure in excess of one hundred fifty thousand."

Kimmel glanced at Ordway. "See to it, Tom. Coordinate some sort of protective measures with the army." He turned back to Forster. "You mentioned a second dispatch."

"Yes, sir. Naval Communications requests that we monitor all Japanese shortwave broadcasts. We're to be on the lookout for something called the 'Winds' code."

"What exactly is the 'Winds' code?"

"I'm not altogether certain, Admiral. Apparently it's some sort of high-level diplomatic code. I gather it would be a signal putting all Japanese embassies on emergency alert."

Kimmel looked disturbed. "How would you interpret such a signal, Commander?"

"Well, sir, I don't think the Japs would go that far unless they meant business. I believe it would be a war signal."

"I agree. Please keep me advised, night or day. I want to know the moment any such intercept occurs."

"Yes, sir." Forster rushed on like a man plunging into cold water. "There's one other thing, Admiral."

"What is it?"

"I would like permission to place the Japanese consulate under surveillance."

There was a moment of shocked silence. The other officers stared at him with a uniform look of astonishment. Then, before Admiral Kimmel could respond, Ordway spoke out.

"Hold on, Forster. Isn't that the purview of the FBI?"

"No, sir," Forster replied. "Not in time of war."

"We're not at war—not yet."

"Perhaps we aren't, but the Japs are. Besides, Admiral, the FBI doesn't have enough men for around-the-clock surveillance. They'll be stretched thin checking out potential saboteurs."

"Point taken," Ordway said with a terse nod. "What are you suggesting?"

"I want to put my own team on stakeout. I'll also need permission for them to operate in civilian clothes."

"And what do you hope to uncover, specifically?"

"Anything would help, sir. According to today's dispatches, we're fast running out of time. I think it's worth a try."

"Very well, permission granted. Unless the Admiral has something else—"

Kimmel shook his head, moving toward the door. Everyone snapped to attention, then Ordway dismissed the meeting. As the officers filed out, he motioned for Forster to remain behind. When the room was clear he turned on Forster with a bulldog scowl. His voice was edged.

"You set me up! Why didn't you bring those dispatches to my attention before the meeting?"

"No harm intended, sir. I just thought it would save time—with Admiral Kimmel present."

"Don't pull it again. And that's an order, mister. So stand advised."

Ordway stalked out the door. For a moment, Forster thought perhaps he'd gone too far. Then, to the empty room, he said what he was really thinking.

"To hell with it."

12

"GOOD MORNING. JAPANESE consulate."
"I beg your pardon?"
"Yes. May I help you?"
"I am calling the Honolulu Ornithological Society."
"So sorry. You have a wrong number."
"Excuse the ring."

Hahn broke the connection. He hung up the phone and walked back to the study. Greta glanced around as he came through the door. He nodded to her questioning look. "Morimura will be notified shortly. Are you almost ready?"

"Only a few minutes more, Eric."

A King James Bible lay opened on the desk. Greta was enciphering a hastily dictated report into codetext. The sheet of typing paper before her was already half-filled with groupings of two-digit numbers. Her pen scratched noisily in the silence.

Hahn watched without comment. His phone call had been prompted by Susan's date with Glenn Lockhart. After debriefing her, he had concluded that the information was critical. The dispatch of fighter planes to Wake Island was, in itself, a revealing move. It underscored the immediacy of the situation.

Until today, Hahn had never contacted the Japanese consulate. His instructions were to resort to the coded phone call only in the event of an emergency. He believed the information in his possession represented nothing less. To wait until his next scheduled report was due might prove a costly mistake. His reference to the Ornithological Society was the key phrase, an instant alert to the consulate switchboard operator. He had every confidence Morimura would appear at Kapiolani Park.

Hahn rose from the desk. He collected his binoculars and walked through the house to the patio. Earlier that morning, he had observed as the *Enterprise* got underway. At the time, he was struck by the fact that the carrier's escort consisted of three heavy cruisers and nine destroyers. Normally, under Standard Operating Procedure, three or four battleships formed the backbone of the escort. He had made a mental note to have Susan check it out.

On the patio, he raised the binoculars and focused on Ford Island. The five battleships he'd seen earlier were still at their moorings. He was about to lower the binoculars when he caught movement out of the corner of his eyes. He quickly focused on the channel and saw the *Lexington* steaming into port. The carrier's escort, which included three battleships, was strung out in a long column down channel. He lowered the binoculars with a look of profound surprise.

All the fleet's battleships were now in Pearl Harbor. Searching his memory, he could recall no instance when the eight dreadnoughts had dropped anchor at the same time. It violated standing SOP, in effect since his arrival in Hawaii. He thought it a vital piece of intelligence, germane to Tokyo's assessment of the Pacific Fleet. He hurried back into the house.

In the study, Hahn dictated an addition to the report. His stress was on the battleships, though he noted the return of the *Lexington*. He promised an update on fleet disposition within the next few days. Greta enciphered the information and transposed it onto the sheet of typing paper. Then she inserted the report behind the front page of the *Honolulu Advertiser*. After collecting her hat and purse, she folded the newspaper under her arm.

"Are you quite certain Morimura will be there?"

"Yes, of course," Hahn said confidently. "The phone call was to be used only in an emergency. I daresay you won't be kept waiting."

"And if he shouldn't arrive? What are your instructions then?"

"Trust me, my dear. Just follow your normal routine and be there by eleven. Nothing will go wrong."

Greta drove straight to the Honolulu Zoo.

She was always somewhat nervous when a drop was scheduled. Her placid nature was ill suited to clandestine meetings, the need for constant vigilance. Today's drop, hastily arranged at the last moment, simply made her all the more apprehensive. But when she stepped out of the car her anxiety quickly diminished. The zoo was swarming with people, mobbed by a morning crush of families and small children. She took comfort in the anonymity of the crowd.

From the zoo she followed the tree-lined path to Kapiolani Park. The walkway was thronged, and people were already spreading picnic blankets on the park's grassy lawns. By the time she reached her usual bench Greta was completely at ease. The bench was empty, and she took that as still another favorable sign. She sat down, placing her purse at her side, then unfolded the newspaper, holding it slightly below eye level. She looked absorbed in the headlines.

At eleven sharp Morimura appeared a short distance down the walkway. Greta saw him and timed her own movements to his approach. She folded the paper, casually placing it on the bench, and gathered her purse. When he was only a few feet away, she rose and walked off toward the zoo. Morimura sat down, legs idly crossed, arms thrown over the back of the bench. Then, pretending to notice the newspaper, he picked it up and began reading. He looked as though he had all the time in the world.

A man paused beside a banyan tree not far from the bench. He was of average height, average build, dressed in an inconspicuous sport coat and slacks. He shook a cigarette from a crumpled pack, then fished a box of matches out of his coat pocket. As he lit up, his eyes shifted rapidly between Morimura and Greta. His expression was a mix of jubilation and indecision. He snuffed the match, exhaling smoke, and his gaze suddenly turned decisive. Strolling past Morimura, he ambled along the path to the zoo. He tailed Greta at a discreet distance.

A knock sounded on the door. Forster looked up from his desk as it swung open. A yeoman stuck his head inside.
"Lieutenant Tucker here to see you, sir."
"Send him in."
Lieutenant Robert Tucker was attired in sport coat and slacks. A native Oklahoman, he was a landlubber who had arrived at Annapolis by way of the scholastic merit tests. He was considerably brighter than he looked, or acted. Forster waved him to a chair.
"What's the problem, Bob? I thought you were on stakeout."
"I was," Tucker said with a slow smile. "Up until about ten-thirty. Then I got lucky."
"Tell me about it."
"You remember our old pal Morimura."
"Yeah?"
"Along about ten-thirty he left the consulate like his pants were on fire. I decided to tail him."
"And?"
"He tried every dodge in the book. Not that he ever spotted me, of course. But he obviously didn't want any uninvited company. I followed him to Kapiolani Park."
"The one down by the zoo?"
Tucker nodded. "Turns out Morimura-san has himself a dead drop. The old park-bench-newspaper-switcheroo gambit. His contact is female, Caucasian, on the sundown side of forty. Looks like your ordinary, everyday housewife."
"Any idea of what she passed him?"
"Nope."

"What did he do then?"

"Beats me," Tucker shrugged. "I followed the woman."

Forster smiled. "You always were crafty."

"Well, Commander, it takes one to know one."

"Okay, get on with it. Where'd she lead you?"

"We made a short stop at the zoo parking lot. She drives the damnedest Cadillac you ever saw."

"You lost her!"

"Today's my day," Tucker grinned. "A taxi showed up with a load of tourists. I told the driver I was Humphrey Bogart. We played detective."

"So where did you end up?"

"Halawa Heights. The lady's house matches her car. One of those showboat cliff-hangers overlooking the ocean."

"Were you able to identify her?"

"Oh, sure. She's got real friendly neighbors."

"What's her name?"

"Greta Hahn," Tucker said without inflection. "Her husband is Dr. Eric Hahn."

Forster sat perfectly still. His head reeled with a sensation not unlike the aftereffects of a monumental drunk. He felt disoriented but only mildy surprised. His growing uncertainty about the Hahn family had proved correct. Yet today's confirmation was more disappointment than triumph. He would have preferred to be wrong.

"No mistake?" he asked Tucker. "You made positive identification?"

"No mistake where the wife is concerned. I can't answer for the rest of the family."

"That's it then. We have to assume they're all involved."

Tucker studied him a moment. "How about the girl? You think she's putting out to get information?"

"You're familiar with Susan Hahn?"

"Everybody at Pearl knows her. You might say she's the talk of the fleet."

"Damn," Forster said. "What a mess."

"How do you want to play it?"

"For the moment, it's just between us. You get on back to the consulate and keep an eye on Morimura. I'll talk to you later."

"You're the skipper."

Tucker flipped him a salute and went out. Forster sat for a long while, deep in reflection. The purpose of Greta Hahn's message drop was all too clear. Morimura and the Japanese Imperial Staff were by now aware of the war alert from Washington. He considered reporting to Ordway, then dismissed the thought. There was no time to wheedle and cajole, seeking authority to act. Nor was there any reason to further complicate matters by involving the brass. He picked up the telephone.

"Operator, connect me with the FBI."

Lamar Moody was Special Agent for the Honolulu office. He was a lean man, with hard eyes and a pleasant smile. His smile today was somewhat strained.

At Forster's request, they had met in the FBI's downtown office. They were on friendly terms, though not friends. So Forster had come straight to the point. He explained the reasons for the stakeout, and went on to describe the results of Tucker's surveillance. He also told Moody everything he knew about Susan Hahn. Then he requested a look at the file on Dr. Eric Hahn.

Moody waited now for him to finish reading. Forster closed the file, silent a moment. His expression was grim. "Not much, is it?"

"Our files on foreign nationals never are. Essentially, it's a record of their activities here, not their native countries."

"Too bad," Forster said in a flat voice. "We may never know whether he's a Nazi agent or just a spy for hire. Not that it makes much difference either way."

"It seems to me your prime concern should be the girl. She's clearly their conduit into Pearl Harbor."

"No question about that. But we can't arrest her without something solid. And we need her to make a case against Morimura and her father."

"What would you like from me?"

"I know you're short on men. So we'll put a surveillance team on the Hahns. And, of course, we'll stick to Morimura like glue."

Moody laughed shortly. "Mr. Hoover would have my neck if he knew about this. By all rights the FBI should be handling the case."

"If we observe the technicalities," Forster remarked, "we're liable to lose the war before it starts. You just don't have the manpower for the job."

"I'm still waiting to hear what you want."

"I'd like you to tap a few phones. The consulate's and Hahn's home for starters."

"No problem," Moody said evenly. "We were planning to tap the consulate and several Jap subversives anyway. We'll just add Hahn to the list."

"I would also appreciate a transcript of all calls."

"Let's talk quid pro quo. We'll cooperate with you down the line. But when the balloon bursts, my office gets credit for the case. Deal?"

"I thought you were worried about Hoover."

"Look at it this way. If you muff it, then I don't know you. And I'll swear on a stack of Bibles that we never had this discussion."

"You're a real patriot, Lamar."

"Every coin has two sides. As an example, I'd wager you're playing a game of your own. Does Admiral Ordway know you're here?"

Forster smiled. "You keep my secrets and I'll keep yours. How's that for a deal?"

"And the girl?"

"I'll deliver her on a silver platter."

They shook hands on it. After Forster left, Moody tilted back in his swivel chair. He steepled his fingers, put his feet up on the desk. It occurred to him that he'd heard only a partial truth. The security of the Pacific Fleet was first and foremost. But it was by no means the crux of the affair. John Forster acted very much as if he had been played for a fool. And one thing was evident in his every word. He wanted the girl for personal reasons. Which meant Susan Hahn was in for a rude awakening. She would soon discover she'd offended the wrong man. And that, Lamar Moody told himself, was a truth within a truth. Perhaps the only truth.

13

ON THURSDAY HAHN took Greta out for lunch. It never occurred to him to look in the rearview mirror. In a plain, black Ford a stout man with jolly features and barracuda eyes tailed Hahn a block or so behind.

Hahn and Greta arrived at the Shunchuro, a popular Japanese restaurant, shortly before twelve. Directly across the highway from Pearl Harbor, the Shunchuro was perched on a steep hillside, which was actually the western slope of an extinct volcano. On a weekday, officers from the base frequently gathered there for lunch. The main gate was less than a five minute drive away.

Greta thought the restaurant a curious choice. Hahn offered no explanation and she refrained from asking questions. But she speculated that he faulted himself for Susan's involvement with Harry Bendix. In retrospect, he clearly felt that her behavior should have alerted him sooner. As for his own performance, he agreed with Morimura's demand for "extraordinary measures." His methods to date had been ordinary and unproductive. He was determined to obtain an aerial photograph of Pearl Harbor.

Today's luncheon was prompted by that resolve. He arranged for a window table, looking westward toward the harbor. The base was on a direct line of sight, scarcely a half mile away. CinCPAC headquarters was clearly visible and, in the distance, warships stood out in bold relief against Ford Island. His hope was that a new perspective would offer some fresh approach to the problem. He needed a stroke of inspiration.

A blazing noonday sun beat down on the harbor. The sky was clear and cloud cover was spotty over the mountains. He stared northward for a long while, inspecting the Koolau Range. Then he looked westward and slowly examined the slopes of the Waianae Range. From those high elevations, it would be possible to take a series of wide lens photographs. Afterwards, with some care, a panoramic montage could be pieced together. But the prospect of scaling those sheer escarpments left him somewhat daunted. He thought it would require the agility of an acrobat and the stamina of a mountain goat. He was neither one.

Their waitress served lunch. His attention diverted from the mountains, he saw the restaurant was now crowded. Fully half the patrons were naval officers, and the irony was inescapable. Their taste for Japanese food, he told himself, would one day return to haunt them. He ate with considerable relish.

Greta picked at her *tempura soba*. She appeared in a ruminative mood. To some extent she was concerned about Morimura's increasing demands. She worried that her husband, in his zeal, would overstep the bounds of prudence. Yet her greater concern was about Susan. She saw the girl's emotional stability hanging by a thread. And she agonized that she'd done nothing to resolve the situation. Her promise weighed heavily.

"Eric," she said abruptly. "I want to talk about Susan."

"What?"

"I've put it off too long. We have to talk about Susan and her young man. You mustn't interfere any—"

"Are you mad?" Hahn rasped. "We are in a public place."

"Parents often discuss their children over lunch. What could be more normal?"

"We will discuss it later . . . at home!"

"No," Greta said calmly. "Now."

"I refuse to listen."

"You have no choice. You will listen and you *will not* attempt to bully me. Shouting in a restaurant would draw attention."

Hahn glared at her owlishly. He saw that he'd been maneuvered into a corner. There was no way to postpone the discussion without creating a scene. He finally nodded.

"Very well." He switched to German, lowering his voice. "What is it you wish to say?"

"I know you, Eric. You are toying with Susan. You bend her to your will by making her suffer."

"Under the circumstances, I thought I was quite generous."

"Only for the moment," Greta remarked. "When it suits your purpose, you will order her to end the relationship. Won't you?"

"I do what I must."

"Not this time, Eric. I won't allow it."

"*You won't—*" Hahn's voice failed him. His features went blood red. "You forget your place. You are my wife, and you will obey me. You will!"

"In all else," Greta said firmly. "But not when it concerns Susan and her young man."

"You talk like a fool. What is this . . . young man . . . to you?"

"We are discussing what he means to Susan. She loves him, and she deserves a little happiness in her life. That is my only interest."

"What about her other . . . young men?"

"She will do as you have instructed. I insist only that she be allowed a private life."

"And when our time here is finished? What happens then? She obviously couldn't remain behind when we leave."

"I worry about today, not tomorrow. Let her have her moment, Eric."

Hahn took out his pipe. Their waitress hovered nearby and he motioned for her to clear the table. He filled his pipe from an oilskin pouch and methodically tamped the tobacco down. When the waitress withdrew, he lit up in a cloud of smoke. His expression was sullen.

"Why do you raise this matter now?"

Greta met his stare. "You ordered Susan to see him only once a week."

"So?"

"She saw him Monday night."

"Please come to the point."

"She plans to go out with him again tomorrow night."

"Nevertheless, that would make twice in one week."

"I told her you would not object."

"You presume to speak for me?"

"Yes, I do. In the future, she will follow your instructions. Tomorrow night is an exception."

"And if I refuse?"

"Then you can find yourself a new courier."

"*What?*"

"Understand me, Eric," Greta said coolly. "I have stated my conditions. Unless you accept, and treat Susan accordingly, then you leave me no choice. I will not participate further in your . . . activities."

"How dare you threaten me!"

"As always, you think only of yourself. Act like a father for a change, think of your daughter." Greta folded her hands on the table, looked at him. "I have nothing more to say, Eric."

By an effort of will, Hahn controlled his rage. She was essential to his mission, and her ultimatum left him no alternative. He decided to play along, let her believe she'd won. Some better solution would present itself in time. And he promised himself she would live to regret today.

"I accede to your wishes, my dear. No great harm will come of Susan's *affaire de coeur*. So perhaps it will all work out for the best."

Greta studied him for a moment. "I hope you mean what you say, Eric."

"But of course I do! You have my word on it."

Hahn smiled benignly, puffing smoke. Then he looked away, his attention diverted by a silvery glint in the sky. He saw a small airplane pass over the restaurant and wing toward Pearl Harbor. It was a civilian monoplane, with fixed landing gear and one propeller. Emblazoned on the fuselage, in bold red letters, was a single word, SIGHTSEEING.

Alert now, Hahn watched as the plane circled the harbor. A moment later the pilot banked sharply and turned his craft toward the windward side. The plane gained altitude and soon vanished across the mountains. Hahn had to suppress a wild urge to laugh out loud. He tapped the dottle from his pipe into an ashtray, then glanced at Greta. His grin was unnaturally wide.

"I have a surprise for you, my dear."

"Oh?"

"Yes indeed! A very pleasant surprise."

Rodgers Airport was southwest of downtown Honolulu. The landing strip, which abutted Keehi Lagoon, serviced inter-island flights and private planes. Offshore was a mooring for the Pan American Clipper.

Hahn parked at the west end of the field. He assisted Greta from the car and they walked toward a hangar. The past hour had been spent in a whirlwind trip home, then to a local photography shop. A Leica camera, loaded with high speed film, dangled from a strap around his neck. His gaze was fixed on a sign over the hangar doorway, TANNEN'S SIGHTSEEING TOURS.

Frank Tannen was a burly man in his late forties. He was bluff and hearty, with a hustler's gift for sizing up a customer. He greeted the Hahns cordially.

"Afternoon, folks. What can I do for you?"

Hahn smiled amiably. "I understand you offer air tours of the island."

"Yes indeedy! Nothing like the view from a thousand feet up. Would you and the missus be interested?"

"What, precisely, does your tour include?"

"Well, first, we'll have a look at Pearl Harbor. Then we'll take a hop over the mountains and see what the natives call the windward side. Then we'll swing back past Diamond Head and Waikiki. Altogether the flight lasts just about an hour."

"And your fee?"

From the accent, Tannen automatically assumed they were tourists. The Leica camera further convinced him that they were wealthy tourists. He looked at them with a guileless smile.

"I see you're a camera bug."

"Oh, yes," Hahn nodded enthusiastically. "It is my one great hobby."

"Well, how's this sound? I'll show you and the missus the island, and get you some terrific photos. All for fifty bucks, satisfaction guaranteed. Okay?"

"That seems very reasonable."

"Well, okay! Just follow me, folks."

Tannen led the way to a Stinson Gullwing. The plane was designed to seat a pilot and four passengers. Greta, looking somewhat dubious about the whole affair, was assisted into the back seat. Hahn took the copilot's seat, positioned beside the starboard window. Within minutes, they were airborne and winging westward.

The driver of the black Ford was parked near the airport terminal. He observed carefully as Tannen loaded his passengers and prepared for takeoff. Then he stepped from the car, shielding his eyes as the plane roared down the runway. A moment later the Stinson banked sharply and winged toward Pearl Harbor. The stout man went in search of a pay phone.

From the air, the Pacific Fleet looked totally different. Hahn's weekly excursions around the harbor had never failed to impress him. But now, peering down from the plane, he saw the entire fleet in one glance. He was struck by the sheer numbers, nearly a hundred warships riding at anchor. There was a formidable aspect about it, like some sleeping colossus. A vague disturbing sense of the invulnerable.

The light was perfect. A cloudless sky, and the sun tilting westerly, made every detail of the harbor sharp and clear. He clicked off an angled shot that encompassed base and harbor. In rapid succession, he focused on CinCPAC headquarters, the submarine pens, and the massive oil storage tanks. Then he photographed the Navy Yard, Battleship Row, and a bird's-eye view of Ford Island. As the plane banked northward, he steadied himself and waited for the exact moment. He got a last panoramic view from an ocean approach.

"How's that?" Tannen bellowed in his ear. "Told you we'd get some terrific shots, didn't I?"

"Perfect, Mr. Tannen. No one could ask for more."

Hahn's smile was genuine. He thought he'd captured on film the very thing needed. A fitting response to Morimura's request. He would remember to use in his report the term *extraordinary measures*.

14

FORSTER ENTERED HIS office at 0700. Earl Bradford walked through the door only moments later. The intelligence analyst looked haggard.

"You'd better brace yourself, John."

"What now?"

"At 0430, the Japs changed call signs."

"Again?" Forster demanded. "You're absolutely certain?"

Bradford dropped into a chair. "No mistake. I double checked the transmission myself. It's from Combined Fleet Headquarters."

"That's twice in one month."

"To be exact, one month to the day. Hardly a coincidence."

"What do you make of it?"

"They're getting ready to do something, and soon. I'd say within the next few days."

"Agreed," Forster said quickly. "But that's not the question. What are they getting ready to do, and where?"

"We had two communiques overnight. One was from British Intelligence. Their planes spotted a Jap task force."

"Headed south?"

Bradford nodded. "Apparently the Japs made rendezvous sometime yesterday. It's a combined invasion group. Battleships, heavy cruisers and troop transports."

"What do you think, Singapore or the Dutch East Indies!"

"I'd say Singapore. If they overrun the British garrison, then there's nothing to stop them. Malaya and the East Indies are goners."

"You didn't mention aircraft carriers."

"I was coming to that. The second dispatch was from Washington. A report from our ambassador in Tokyo finally filtered down to Naval Intelligence."

"And it's all bad news?"

"The worst," Bradford acknowledged. "Until the night of November 30, both carrier divisions were anchored in Tankan Bay. The next morning they were gone and they haven't been sighted since. They just disappeared."

"Any indication of when they arrived in Tankan Bay?"

"November 19."

"Which was the day we lost radio contact. And they've maintained radio silence ever since."

"Add that to today's change in call signs and you've got a real problem. It appears they're preparing to strike in three places simultaneously."

There was a moment of calculation before Forster spoke. "Let's assume one of the carrier divisions will hit the Philippines. MacArthur has almost three hundred planes to throw against an invasion force. So the Japs definitely need air strike capability."

"Correct."

"So where does that leave the other carrier division?"

"Good question," Bradford said, wrapped in thought. "We can forget Singapore, even Wake and Midway. None of those would require an entire carrier division."

"What else is left? What threatens the Japs so much that they would commit six carriers?"

"By process of elimination, only one thing."

"Go ahead, say it out loud."

"The Pacific Fleet."

"The unimaginable and the unspeakable, all rolled into one."

"Only for Washington," Bradford observed. "For the Japs, it makes a crazy kind of sense. Hit us here and they won't have to fight us at sea. You might call it the lesser of two evils."

Forster leaned forward, hands clasped on the desktop. "Yesterday I got a call from Joe Michaels. He's one of the team assigned to the Hahn family."

"What are they up to?"

Forster briefly related the story. He explained that he'd ordered Michaels to interview the owner of the plane. In the course of questioning Floyd Tannen, he'd made a startling discovery about Dr. Hahn's first sightseeing tour.

"So I asked myself," Forster chuckled. "Why would the Japs want aerial photographs of Pearl? The obvious answer was even too much for me . . . until a minute ago."

Bradford shook his head. "We'll never convince Ordway or anyone else. It sounds like looney-tunes logic, unless you're a Jap."

"Holy Jumping — !"

"What?"

"The study you made on the Japs. You know, how they always move to secure their flanks."

"Yeah?"

"Anything in there that would support our argument?"

"As a matter of fact, there was a good deal of correlated material I left out. It wasn't central to the premise of the study. But it's damn sure relevant now."

"Get it! Everything you've got, Earl. The works!"

Bradford was galvanized to action. Forster watched him race out the door, then slowly unclasped his hands. He realized his palms were sweating, while at the same time his mouth felt dry as dust. He recognized the symptoms from his football days at Annapolis. A case of pregame jitters, otherwise known as butterflies. And today his opponent wore gold braid.

"*Pearl Harbor!*"

Admiral Thomas Ordway's mouth dropped open. He stared at Forster with a look of genuine amazement. A moment passed before he was able to collect himself.

"Preposterous," he finally grated. "Why would the Japs do a crazy thing like that?"

"Because we showed them how, Admiral. We blueprinted it and proved it would work."

"I presume you're talking about the Joint Services report?"

In March, a joint Army-Navy study had been released. The report asserted that Japan, prior to formal declaration of war, might launch a surprise air attack on Pearl Harbor. Further, the report concluded that a dawn attack, launched from carriers offshore, could achieve complete surprise. The study, although secret, had been widely quoted in military publications.

"The report," Forster answered in a low voice, "was the blueprint. We proved it was feasible almost ten years ago." He placed a bound volume on Ordway's desk. "Here's a summary of Joint Exercise Number Four. You'll note it's dated Sunday, February 7, 1932."

Ordway riffled the pages. "Wasn't that the war games exercise involving the *Lexington* and the *Saratoga*?"

"Yes, sir," Forster replied. "The carriers launched their aircraft before daylight, from a point one hundred miles northeast of Oahu. You'll recall they achieved total surprise. Our Air Corps was caught flat footed."

"I also recall there was a disclaimer. The attack force was limited strictly to bombs. Torpedoes were ruled out because the harbor's too shallow. War games, Commander, are not the same as war."

"I respectfully disagree, sir. The British attacked the Italian Fleet in Taranto Harbor a year ago November. They sank three battleships with aerial torpedoes adapted for shallow water. And I'd lay odds the message wasn't lost on the Japs."

"Perhaps not," Ordway remarked stiffly. "On the other hand, you're asking me to believe a phantom carrier division is steaming toward Hawaii. Isn't that the gist of it?"

"It's no phantom, Admiral."

"I stand corrected. But you've nonetheless lost contact. You haven't the foggiest where those carriers are right now, do you?"

"No, sir."

"Then I suggest you report back to me when you find them."

"Admiral, I think they'll find us before we find them."

"That's all, Commander."

Forster was on his way downstairs before he remembered the Hahn incident. He stopped, tempted to return and buttress his argument with actual proof. Then, reluctantly, he was forced to admit that his proof involved a family of spies. Not a carrier division. He walked back to his office.

Greta left the house at ten-thirty. On the car seat beside her was a copy of the morning newspaper. Below Halawa Heights, she stopped for gas at a roadside service station. Then she drove toward Honolulu. She was aware that today's report was far from routine. Every item she'd enciphered into the report, and what was revealed by the photographs, seemed equally disturbing. She thought the Americans were marvelously well organized. And frighteningly alert.

Her husband's zeal frightened her even more. She considered yesterday's plane ride foolhardy and rashly imprudent, and afterwards he had turned a deaf ear to her protests. She nonetheless remained convinced that he'd made a mistake. The pilot would remember and perhaps begin to wonder. Curiosity bred suspicion.

As she drove she reflected on the change in her husband's attitude. Before, he'd been dedicated to the mission, shrewdly determined. But now he seemed like a man pitted in a race against time. He was pressing, taking unnecessary risks, as though the clock would stop at any moment. Worse, he was intoxicated with his own daring, utterly cocksure. He believed himself immune to mistake or exposure, and that was what frightened her the most. No man was infallible.

Approaching the zoo, she forced herself to put the thought

from her mind. There were few people in sight, and the parking lot was all but empty. Her nerves took a sharp uptick, and she once more felt that leaden sense of apprehension. As she stepped from the car, she silently wished for the anonymity of Saturday's crowds. Then, chiding her own fears, she gathered her purse and tucked the thickened newspaper under her arm. She walked off toward the park.

On the street, Joe Michaels pulled over to the curb a block away from the zoo. His orders were to keep his distance should the Hahn woman attempt another drop. Bob Tucker, who was tailing Morimura, would enter the park and verify that an exchange had taken place. When the woman returned to her car, Michaels would then resume his surveillance. He lit a cigarette and settled down to wait.

The drop site was the same as usual. Greta seated herself on the bench, pretending interest in the headlines. A minute or so before eleven she saw Morimura approaching from the direction of the beach. She placed the paper on the bench, rose with her purse in hand, and walked away. Morimura moved directly to the bench and sat down. He picked up the paper, unfolding it to the front page, and held it canted slightly downward. His eyes were on the man who had followed him.

Only moments earlier, he had become aware of the man while crossing the beach. He automatically assumed the FBI had placed him under surveillance because of the confirmed war alert. He watched now as the man moved to a bench farther down the walkway and took a seat. His mind was a jumble of thoughts, but one thing seemed uppermost. He could not allow himself to be arrested.

It was imperative that he return to the consulate and transmit the information to Tokyo. Yet, with the coded message and photographs in his possession, it was absolutely imperative that he not be taken into custody. His own arrest, followed swiftly by the arrest of the Hahn family, perhaps even the Consul General as well would result in disaster for Japan. It was, without question, unacceptable.

One other factor occurred to him. So far as he knew, he hadn't been followed before today. In that event, only one man could identify Greta Hahn as the woman who made the drop. His gaze flicked to the man seated on the distant bench. Then he quickly scanned the park and saw no one else in sight. His decision was made without hesitation, for there seemed no alternative. He took a moment to work out the moves in his mind.

Folding the newspaper, Morimura got to his feet. He casually strolled away, turning onto the path leading to the zoo. He kept his gaze fixed straight ahead, resisting the temptation to glance over his shoulder. He was certain the man would follow.

A short ways farther on, the tree-lined path curved abruptly. Morimura waited until he was around the bend, momentarily out of sight. Then he stepped off the path and positioned himself behind the trunk of a banyan tree. He pulled a switchblade knife from his pants pocket and pressed the release button. The blade sprang open.

Several moments passed in tense silence. Then he heard the crunch of footsteps, drawing closer to the twist in the path. He timed it perfectly, stepping around the tree at the exact instant the man turned the curve. His arm pistoned upward, and he drove the knife through a spot below the sternum bone. The man coughed a grunt of surprise as the blade punctured his heart. His eyes suddenly went blank and he dropped dead.

Morimura knelt beside the corpse. He retrieved the knife and hurriedly lifted the dead man's wallet. He was about to take the watch as well when he saw the Annapolis class ring. His features blanched in a look of startled comprehension. He stood and swiftly walked away.

15

FORSTER RETURNED TO the base late that evening. From the Honolulu City Morgue, where he'd spent the last four hours, he drove straight to CinCPAC headquarters. His expression was brutalized cold hard rage.

Lieutenant Joe Michaels was waiting in his office. Forster nodded curtly and seated himself behind the desk. He unbuttoned his tunic, loosening his tie with a sharp tug. Then he lit a cigarette, exhaling smoke as he snapped the lighter closed. He glanced up at Michaels.

"I got the body released."

"What took so long?"

"The coroner and the police wanted to argue about it. They weren't too keen on the idea."

"You mean surrendering the body to Navy custody?"

"Yeah," Forster said wearily. "That and putting the lid on their investigation. Cops don't like to turn loose of a murder case."

"How'd you convince them?"

"I called in Lamar Moody. He told them the FBI and the Navy are working on a matter involving national security. They weren't happy, but they went along."

"What about the newspapers?"

"The police issued a statement calling it robbery-murder. Nothing was said about Tucker's Naval Intelligence ID. He carried that separate from his wallet, and the man who found him didn't touch the body. So the coroner's report will read 'victim unknown.' "

"Who found him?"

"Some guy taking a noontime walk through the park."

Forster paused, took a long drag on his cigarette. "All right, let's get to your story. Tell me exactly what you saw."

"Not much," Michaels replied. "The Hahn woman left her car in the zoo parking lot at ten-forty-eight. She returned at eleven-o-five and drove back home. I tailed her all the way."

"How did she act when she came out of the park?"

"I'd say pretty normal. She didn't look panicky or anything."

"Then we could assume she wasn't involved in the killing."

"That would be my guess."

"And you never saw Morimura?"

"No. I stayed in my car the whole time.'

"In other words, no witnesses," Forster said thoughtfully. "Morimura probably figured Bob was the only one who'd seen the woman. With him dead, we wouldn't have a lead to the Hahn family. Or so Morimura thought."

"What now? Do we pick up Morimura?"

Forster shook his head. "We still haven't got anything on the girl. And we have to implicate her before we'll get the others. She's the cog in their wheel."

"Only one trouble. Morimura will be very leery about message drops now. He knows he's under surveillance."

"It doesn't matter. Whatever code they're using, we'd never break it from a single message. We need the girl to make a case."

"So how do you plan to nail her?"

"I wish I knew."

"Why not just grab the whole bunch. We'd at least short-circuit their transmissions to Tokyo."

"It won't work. Any night-school lawyer could get the Hahns

out on a writ of habeas corpus. As for Morimura, we couldn't touch him without hard evidence. He would just claim diplomatic immunity."

"Damn Jap! I wish I'd been in the park instead of Bob. I would've shoved that knife up—"

"I'll think of something, Joe. You and your team just keep me informed on the Hahns. And that goes double for the girl."

"Wherever she goes, Commander, we go."

Michaels withdrew, closing the door on his way out. Forster took a final drag on his cigarette, squashed it in an ashtray. He scrubbed his face hard with his hands, fighting fatigue. Then, suddenly, he remembered another disagreeable task. He still had to report to Ordway.

On impulse, he decided to wait until morning. He wanted his wits about him, for he intended to lie by omission. Ordway would be told that Lieutenant Tucker had been murdered while tailing a member of the Japanese Consulate. Further, he would be informed that an investigation, in cooperation with the FBI, was already underway. But there would be no mention of the Hahns, or the existence of an entrenched spy ring. Forster wanted no interference until . . . .

A sharp image passed before his eyes. For an instant he was back at the morgue, looking down as the sheet was drawn from Bob Tucker's head. The vision was like a live electric wire touched to his nerve ends. His fatigue vanished, replaced once again by cold rage. He put his mind to formulating some new plan. A more direct line of action.

He closed his eyes and thought of Susan Hahn.

Aboard the *Nevada* gunnery drills were conducted every day. Harry Bendix and the Battery Officer stood behind the starboard secondary battery. The crews manning the 5-inch guns were alert and poised, as though awaiting the start of a race. Bendix held a stopwatch in his hand.

Amidships, on the platform deck, the crew of the fire control director was plotting a mock setup. The Fire Control Officer looked on while operators determined bearing, elevation, and range of an aircraft target. Compensation for wind drift, as well as angle of lead, was calculated into the setup. All these factors were then relayed to the starboard secondary battery. With the setup plotted, the Fire Control Officer began speaking into the microphone of his headset.

Bendix started his stopwatch as the gun crews moved into action. At each station, the gun was elevated and brought onto the correct azimuth by following the signals from fire control. Beside the gun platform, the third loader manhandled a box of dummy ammo into position. The second loader pulled shells from the box and placed them nose-down in the fuze pot, which set the mechanical fuze. Last in line, the first loader then swung a shell from the fuze pot onto a rack directly beneath the gun chamber. An instant later the gun captain shoved a compressed air lever and the shell was rammed home. The breechblock closed with a thud.

"Time!" Bendix clicked the stopwatch. "Eight seconds on the button. Not bad, but not good enough. Standby!"

Gunnery drills went on throughout the day. First thing every morning Bendix inspected the secondary battery, a total of sixteen 5-inch guns scattered about the ship. Before lunch, he checked out the seventy-six pom-pom guns of the antiaircraft battery. Every afternoon he conducted drills with the huge 16-inch guns of the main battery, six forward and three aft. This morning he was less than pleased with the starboard secondary battery. Eight seconds was not his idea of teamwork.

"Sir."

Bendix turned to find an orderly at his elbow. "What is it?"

"Message from the Exec Officer, sir. You are to report immediately to Commander Forster, CinCPAC headquarters. The captain's launch will take you ashore."

"Did the Exec say what it's about?"

"No, sir. That's the entire message."

"Tell him I'm on my way."

"Aye, aye, sir."

Bendix ordered the Battery Officer to take over the drills. Then he hurried amidships and went down the gangway. As he clambered aboard the waiting launch, he puzzled on the somewhat cryptic message. He couldn't imagine what business he had with John Forster, or Naval Intelligence.

"How about a cup of coffee?"

"No thanks, Commander."

"Cigarette?"

"Never use them."

"So you don't. I guess I forgot."

Forster shook a cigarette from a pack on his desk. He lit up and studied Bendix through a haze of smoke. His expression was neutral.

"You must be wondering why I sent for you."

"I'll have to admit I'm curious."

"Well, first, let me say that it's just between us. Your skipper will be told only what he needs to know. And I guarantee he won't ask questions."

Bendix inclined his head. "Sounds serious."

"Dead serious. And that's why I need your help."

"What kind of help could I provide Naval Intelligence?"

Forster paused, flicked an ash off his cigarette. "What I'm about to tell you is top secret. It's not to be repeated outside this room."

"Yes, sir."

"Simply put," Forster said quietly, "I have reason to believe the Japs are preparing to attack Pearl Harbor."

"Pearl!" Bendix echoed. "Are you sure?"

"All of our intelligence points in that direction. We believe the attack will be launched from carriers, and soon. Sometime within the next week or ten days."

"Even so, Commander. How can I—?"

"Let me explain. Our immediate problem is a spy ring here on Oahu. It's operated by a member of the Japanese Consulate. His name is Takeo Morimura."

"I'll be damned."

"Yesterday one of my men was murdered. He had the bad luck to witness a meeting between Morimura and a clandestine agent. He was knifed to death in Kapiolani Park."

Bendix appeared perplexed. "I still don't get it. Where do I fit into the picture?"

"You're acquainted with the clandestine agent."

"I am?"

"Her name is Greta Hahn."

"What?"

"Her husband, Dr. Eric Hahn, answers directly to Morimura. We suspect he's a trained Nazi agent — on loan to the Japanese."

"I don't believe it!"

"His daughter," Forster went on in a monotone, "is their most valuable agent. Her responsibility is to report on Pearl Harbor and the Pacific Fleet."

"You're daffy! There's been a foul-up somewhere."

"I'm sorry to say it's all true. She played you for a chump, Bendix."

"Like hell!" Bendix flared. "I wasn't born yesterday. You think I don't know when a woman's on the level?"

"Not this one," Forster said deliberately. "She's screwing five other guys besides you. Would you like their names?"

"No."

"All right. Suffice it to say she's covered the fleet. I have an idea you knew she was sleeping around — didn't you?"

Bendix looked beaten. A pulse throbbed in his neck and for a moment he sat immobilized, as though frozen in place. Then he passed a hand over his eyes. His voice was phlegmy.

"What do you want, Forster?"

"I understand you asked her to marry you."

Bendix looked at him in stony silence.

"I also understand she turned you down. So that explains why you look so glum whenever you two are together. But tell me about Susan. What's her problem?"

"Believe it or not," Bendix said dismally, "she does love me. If she strung me along, it's because of her father. Whatever she's done, he forced her to do. You'll never convince me otherwise."

"On the contrary, I hope you're right. It would make things a whole lot simpler."

"What things?"

Forster stubbed out his cigarette. "I want you to work on her. Drop a few hints that we're about to crack a major spy ring. Let her know we'll consider amnesty for anyone who turns informant." He paused a beat. "I need airtight proof that the Japs plan to attack. And I need it fast."

"Forget it," Bendix said flatly. "You're asking me to put her head on the block."

"I'm not asking," Forster said, a touch of iron in his voice. "I'm ordering you. We're not talking about your love life, Bendix. We're talking about your country."

"Christ. You're a cold fish, aren't you, Forster?"

"I do what I have to — and so will you."

Bendix seemed to slump forward in his chair. His head bowed and his expression was one of absolute resignation. He spoke with his eyes on the floor.

"Do you mean it about amnesty?"

"You get her to talk and I'll do my damnedest. You have my word on it, Harry."

"Where do I start? How do you *hint* about something like that?"

Forster smiled and lit another cigarette. Then he told him.

16

"Hello."
"Mrs. Hahn?"
"Yes."
"Harry Bendix here. How are you today?"
"Very well, thank you."
"I wonder, could I speak with Susan?"
"Hold on a moment. I'll just go and—"
Susan entered from the hallway. Her eyes were still heavy with sleep and she wore a peignoir over her nightgown. She looked as though she'd spent a restless night. Greta extended the phone.
"It's your young man."
"Harry?"
Greta nodded and turned away. Susan waited until she went through the door to the dining room. Then she answered in a low voice.
"What a pleasant surprise."
"Hi." He sounded somehow harried. "Look, I hate to put you on the spot and I apologize. But I really need to see you tonight."
"Oh, I couldn't, Harry. We were out last night. Father would have a fit."
"Work it out somehow. You know I wouldn't ask if it weren't important."
"Is anything wrong?"

"Yes and no. I can't talk about it now. I'll tell you tonight."

Susan hesitated briefly. She sensed he wasn't quite himself, and that worried her. "All right," she said reluctantly. "But don't come here. I'll call Kathryn and arrange a ride. We can meet at the club."

"Great! I knew you could do it."

"If it were anyone else—"

"Listen, I've got to run. I only came ashore to call you. Seven o'clock okay?"

"Fine."

When they hung up Susan placed a call to the base. She left a message for Tom Gordon, canceling their date that evening. She was about to call Kathryn when she remembered they were scheduled to attend the weekly bridge club meeting. She decided to wait and make the arrangements then.

In the kitchen she poured herself a cup of coffee. Greta was busy kneading dough and didn't look around. Susan moved to the counter, watching for a time in silence. Finally, she concluded her mother was waiting for her to speak. She saw no reason for pretense.

"I'm going to see Harry tonight, Mama."

Greta continued kneading. "What will you tell your father?"

"A white lie. What he doesn't know won't hurt him."

"Be very careful with lies. Your father's temper is not good these days."

"Well, that's certainly nothing new, Mama!"

Greta slapped the dough a hard whack. She stopped and glanced up at Susan. "Listen closely to what I say. Do not allow your father to catch you in lies. I could not protect you then."

"Protect me?"

"Do you want to continue seeing your young man?"

"Of course."

"Then just do as I say. No questions."

Greta went back to kneading the dough. Susan stared at her, more fearful than ever before. She realized she'd been told something without the words being spoken. Her mother, at some point in time, had intervened on her behalf. She was afraid to ask the reason, even more frightened of what the answer might reveal. She didn't want to know.

She kissed her mother quickly and walked from the kitchen.

Bendix was waiting in the parking lot that evening. He approached the car as Kathryn pulled into an empty space. Susan noted he was dressed in civilian clothes, which automatically ruled out the club. She assumed he wanted to be alone.

Kathryn was the perfect conspirator. She exchanged greetings with Bendix but asked no questions. He assisted Susan out of the car, and they crossed the parking lot as Kathryn walked toward the club. A moment later they drove off in his convertible.

At the main gate Bendix took the road to Honolulu. He casually mentioned that he'd made reservations on the windward side. Susan was delighted with the arrangement, quite content to have him to herself. Their moments together were so precious that she'd come to resent the crowds at the Officers' Club. She was happiest when they were by themselves.

On the way into town Bendix was quieter than normal. All day he'd tried to prepare himself for the task ahead. But now that he was with her, his ambivalence was like a stone in the pit of his stomach. He felt trapped between love on the one hand, and duty to his country on the other. He had deep misgivings about tonight, and he wasn't at all sure he could pull it off. It still seemed impossible that she was a spy.

"Now tell me," she said as they turned toward the mountains. "What was so important about tonight?"

"I wanted to see you."

"Actually, you said you *needed* to see me. And when I asked if anything was wrong, you said yes and no. Why all the mystery?"

Bendix shrugged. "The only mystery is when I sail. Our skipper expects orders at any time."

"I thought this was your week in port."

"Have you forgotten we're on standby alert?"

"How could I? No one talks about anything else."

"Yeah, I know. The whole fleet is trying to outguess the Japs. Where will they strike and when? That's the big question."

"What makes everyone think they will strike?"

"Not everyone does. Lots of people think it's all a load of nonsense."

She hesitated a moment. "And you?"

"I'm convinced the Japs are planning to hit the Philippines. When they do, yours truly will be out to sea for a month of Sundays. That's why I said I *needed* to see you tonight."

"But . . ." she faltered, quickly went on. "You believe it could happen soon, then?"

"I think it's strictly hour by hour. And I'd like to spend the last hour with you."

Susan murmured an inaudible reply. She hugged his arm and put her head on his shoulder. Until now, she'd never considered the possibility that he would be involved in the fighting. She thought perhaps she had blocked it out of her mind. Something too terrible to contemplate, or confront. Suddenly, though, it was all too real. And she was devastated by the realization that he might be killed. She felt sick at heart.

The conversation waned. For the balance of the drive, they both seemed absorbed in their own thoughts. Their destination was the oriental inn on Kaneohe Bay. They were shown to the same private room, and their meal was served by the young native girl who had waited on them before. After dinner, the girl cleared the table and returned with a bottle of brandy. She once more bid them a sly goodnight.

Bendix lounged back on the cushy pillows. As the sliding door swished shut, his gaze drifted to the window. He was silent for a time, staring out at the moonlit sea. Finally, he swigged his brandy and glanced around at Susan. His voice was halting.

"Wonder if the saboteurs are at work tonight."

"What saboteurs?"

"Haven't you heard the latest?"

"Apparently not."

"Well, I got it straight from the horse's mouth. On the way to the club, I ran into John Forster. He gave me the lowdown."

"On the saboteurs?"

"Among other things." Bendix suddenly looked uncomfortable. "According to Forster, the saboteurs are just the tip of the iceberg. He says they're controlled by a Jap spy ring."

"Oh?"

"That's what he told me. A Jap spy ring with undercover agents and the whole works. Hard to believe, but Forster ought to know if anybody does. I mean, after all, he's in the spy business."

For a sliver of eternity Susan stared at him. The expression in his eyes touched her heart with a cold chill. She knew John Forster would never have confided in him or anyone else. So everything he'd just said was a lie. She steadied herself and went along with the charade. She sensed there was more to come.

"What brought the subject up?"

Bendix gave her a hangdog look. "Forster's feeling pretty proud of himself. To hear him tell it, he's about to crack the spy ring. I guess he just wanted a sounding board."

"Pardon me?"

"You know, a good listener. Someone who'll give an objective opinion."

"Oh, I see. John wanted your opinion on something to do with the spy ring?"

"Yeah, more or less. He needs an inside witness to really break the case. So he's willing to offer amnesty to anyone who will turn informant. He asked me what I thought."

"And what was your reply?"

"It ought to work," Bendix said with downcast eyes. "I told him anyone with any sense would jump at the offer. When the choice is amnesty or a firing squad — it's no choice at all."

"Where does John hope to find an informant?"

"I suppose it's a matter of getting the word to the right person. He'll figure a way to do it somehow."

Susan tried to keep her tone light. "If I know John, he's probably already thought of some clever gambit. Will you excuse me a minute, Harry? I have to powder my nose."

Bendix appeared startled by her abrupt loss of interest. She patted his cheek and rose, moving through the sliding door. Outside, she hurried down the corridor to the ladies' room. Only a thread of her composure remained as she closed the door and locked it. Her hands suddenly began to shake.

She fumbled a handkerchief from her pocketbook. At the sink she turned on the tap, and patted her face with cold water. The trembling subsided, and she slowly pulled herself together. She kept the damp cloth pressed to her forehead while she considered what seemed a hopeless situation. The truth left her numbed.

Harry knew everything. His awkward manner indicated he was an unwilling pawn. But it was all too clear that Forster had somehow persuaded him to act as an intermediary. How much Forster could actually prove was another matter entirely. Without an informant, he was apparently hesitant to move against the intelligence network. Otherwise he would never have extended an offer of clemency. So her options were clear.

By betraying her entire family, she could save herself. It was an idea she rejected out of hand. She would not be a party to the imprisonment, perhaps the execution, of her own parents. The alternative, then, was to play out the game until they were all caught. For she saw now what she'd never before allowed herself to consider, much less admit. Arrest was inevitable.

A strange sense of loss came over her. Not for herself or her parents, regardless of whatever unpleasantness awaited them. But rather the loss of what she'd found with Harry Bendix. Her old fatalism, once more shorn of hope, quickly asserted herself. She would live one day at a time until there was no more time. And her one last hope, almost a prayer, was that Harry would be willing to share whatever time remained. The end might yet be postponed a while longer.

After checking her makeup, she lightly dabbed herself with perfume. She walked up the hall and eased through the sliding door. When Bendix looked around, she somehow managed a smile that was at once warm and alluring. She sat down beside him as though nothing had happened to mar their night together. Her eyes were luminous, without regret or pain. She gently took his face in her hands.

"I love you, Harry."

"Oh God, Susan!"

"No, we won't talk of anything else. Not tonight, not ever again."

Her arms went around him and she pulled him tightly to her breast. "If you still want me, I'm yours, Harry. I'll always be yours."

"You know I do," he whispered, his voice tight with strain. "I'll want you no matter—"

"Shhh."

She hushed him softly, then kissed him on the mouth. He groaned, and his arms encircled her like bands of steel.

17

"I ORDERED YOU to report here at o-eight hundred."

Bendix stood at attention. He hadn't been asked to sit and his eyes were fixed on a spot just above Forster's head. He said nothing now.

"Well, speak up," Forster demanded. "Why did you make me send for you? It's almost ten."

"I had gunnery drills scheduled."

"Don't try to jerk me around, Bendix. And put a 'sir' on the end of that."

"I had gunnery drills . . . *sir*."

"You know damn well my orders supersede your normal duties. I made that clear the other day. Now, why didn't you report here this morning?"

"No excuse, sir."

There was a sullen, somewhat mulish expression on Bendix's face. For a moment, Forster stared at him across the desk. He saw that an adversary relationship would lead nowhere. Nor would pulling rank produce a spirit of cooperation. He decided on another tack.

"All right, Harry," He motioned to a chair. "Let's talk off the cuff, man to man. What's the problem?"

Bendix sat down. "No problem. I didn't report because I don't have anything to tell."

"Nothing?"

"Nothing worth repeating."

"Suppose you let me be the judge of that. What happened?"

"I made your offer. No names, no reference to her father. I used the roundabout approach you suggested."

"And?"

"She wasn't interested."

"What did she say?"

"Nothing."

"C'mon, Harry. Quit making me pull teeth. She must have said something."

"She acted like it was all news to her."

"No questions? She didn't ask how we'd tumbled to them? How the amnesty would work?"

"Not a word. She just heard me out and then she went to the restroom. When she came back, it was like nothing had happened."

"The restroom." Forster paused, gave him an appraising look. "What was her mental condition? Tell me exactly how she reacted."

"I've already told you. She didn't react one way or the other."

"Was she aware the offer was directed at her?"

Bendix's voice dropped. "She understood."

"How can you be sure?"

"Something she said when she came back from the restroom. Or maybe the way she said it."

"So she said something after all. What was it?"

"In so many words, she told me to forget the amnesty. She said we shouldn't talk about anything but ourselves."

"Now we're getting somewhere. However she phrased it, she actually refused the offer. Affirmative?"

"Yeah, I guess so."

"What happened then?"

"That was it, end of discussion."

"Oh?" Forster said skeptically. "You must have talked about

something. You didn't leave that oriental joyshack till almost three this morning."

"You had us followed?"

"Grow up, Harry. I have the whole family under surveillance."

"Goddamnit!" Bendix exploded. "She was with me. You have no business poking around in private . . . things."

"Your privacy is strictly second fiddle. I'm trying to deep six a spy ring. Or did she make you forget that?"

Bendix squared himself up. His face was white with anger and perspiration suddenly beaded his forehead. His hands were knotted into fists.

"I want out," he said roughly. "I tried and she turned me down. Get someone else to do your dirty work."

"Are you saying you're through with Susan? You won't see her again?"

"Just keep your Peeping Toms off my heels. I don't put on a sideshow for anyone — you included!"

"Then you do plan on seeing her again?"

"I might and I might not."

"How did you leave it with her last night?"

"None of your business."

Forster stiffened. There was an impenetrable hardness in his eyes, something beyond anger. His tone was quiet, oddly matter of fact.

"Harry, your girlfriend's a spy. You don't have any doubt of that now, do you?"

Bendix eyed him warily. "No."

"On the other hand, her feelings toward you are apparently genuine. Otherwise, she would have given you a quick brushoff last night. Correct?"

"I suppose so."

"Okay, don't think about my next question. Just tell me what your instinct tells you. Would she spill the beans about last night to her father?"

"No, I don't believe she would. I got the impression she just wanted to forget it ever happened."

"Good," Forster nodded. "If you're right, then she's waffling between loyalty to her family and what she feels for you. And that means we still have a chance."

"I won't do it!" Bendix bristled. "She asked me to let it drop and I agreed. So that's that."

"Oh, you'll do it, Harry. Shall I tell you why?"

Bendix glared at him in cold silence.

"There are two reasons. First, she wouldn't turn informant for anyone else. She still might for you."

"And the second reason."

"If you refuse to try," Forster said in a low, dangerous voice, "and the Japs attack, then all bets are off. I'll personally guarantee that Susan goes to the gallows."

"Forster, you must have ice water in your veins."

Bendix slammed the door on his way out. Forster wasn't proud of himself, but he'd made the threat in earnest. Thus far, his every effort had proved futile. The FBI phone taps had uncovered nothing of an incriminating nature. Even worse, Morimura had easily eluded surveillance last night. The likelihood was that he would do so again and again, whenever he pleased. Simply knowing he was being tailed gave him every advantage.

So Susan Hahn really was the last chance. And it was a chance that dimmed with each passing hour. He in no way regretted the threat.

6 DECEMBER 1941
FROM: ONI
ACTION: CINCPAC NAVIT
HIGHLY RELIABLE INFORMATION RECEIVED THAT URGENT INSTRUCTIONS FROM TOKYO WERE SENT YESTERDAY TO JAPANESE DIPLOMATIC AND CONSULAR POSTS AT WASHINGTON, MANILA, HONOLULU, LONDON, HONG KONG, AND SINGAPORE TO DESTROY THEIR CODES AND CIPHERS, AND TO BURN ALL OTHER CONFIDENTIAL AND SECRET DOCUMENTS.

Forster carefully spread the dispatch on his desk. He lit a cigarette, aware that he wasn't at all surprised. The order from Tokyo was standard procedure for any country preparatory to war. As for the list of embassies and consulates, it merely reaffirmed what he'd suspected all along. America and Great Britain were about to be attacked.

Studying the dispatch, he was nonetheless intrigued by the opening words. "Highly reliable information" was clearly the result of another "Magic" intercept. The cloak and dagger bunch in Washington, particularly the Office of Naval Intelligence, still wouldn't admit they'd broken Japan's diplomatic code. He wondered what else "Magic" had told them and intelligence never passed along. He cursed them for doling out the information in drops and driblets. It was no way to prepare for war.

Forster delayed reporting to Admiral Ordway. The ONI dispatch raised a question he knew he would be asked. Before going upstairs, he thought it best to talk with Allan White, the Lieutenant j.g. who now headed the Honolulu Consulate surveillance team. Since Bob Tucker's murder, the team leaders were under standing orders to call him every day at noon. The first call today, at twelve sharp, was from Joe Michaels. He reported no signs of unusual activity at the Hahn home. A minute or so later Al White called.

"How's it going, Al?"

"Quiet as a church, sir. Morimura hasn't put his head outside all morning."

"Keep your eyes open. He's trickier than he looks."

"Yes, sir, I will."

"All right, let me ask you about something else. Does the consulate have a fireplace chimney?"

"Funny you'd mention that, Commander."

"Why?"

"We spotted smoke early yesterday evening and again this morning. We've been wondering why they built a fire. I mean, it hasn't rained or anything. So there's no chill in the air."

"When did the smoke stop?"

"It hasn't. The fire was still going when I left to call you."

"Stick with it, Al. I'll talk to you later."

Forster hurried out of his office. Upstairs, he caught Ordway preparing to leave for lunch. The admiral grudgingly accepted the ONI dispatch and read it through. He looked up with a bemused expression.

"I take it you attach some significance to all this?"

"Yes, sir," Forster said without caution. "I believe it's the equivalent of a war alert. The tip-off is the location of the embassies and consulate."

"British and American?"

"Exactly, Admiral. Tokyo wouldn't order those code books destroyed without a reason. I think an all-out Jap offensive is imminent — a matter of days."

"Perhaps so," Ordway allowed. "However, that's hardly news. Our last assessment from Naval Operations indicates as much."

"Yes, sir, but only with regard to Singapore and the Philippines. There's still no mention of Pearl Harbor."

"Come now, Forster. We've been through that before. Why beat a dead horse?"

"Admiral, the consulate in town started burning code books yesterday evening. They're still at it this morning."

"How do you know?"

"Our surveillance team spotted smoke from the fireplace chimney. We didn't make the connection until I received ONI's dispatch."

"So?" Ordway asked crossly. "How does that support your theory about Pearl? If the Japs attack the Philippines, we would automatically occupy the Honolulu consulate. Isn't that correct?"

"Yes, sir."

"Then what more explanation do you need? The code books are being burned to prevent them from falling into our hands. It certainly doesn't signal an attack on the Pacific Fleet."

Forster was at an impasse. His frustration boiled over and he suddenly decided he'd delayed too long. It was time to put the cards on the table.

"Admiral, are you familiar with Dr. Eric Hahn?"

"Only as a nodding acquaintance. I've seen him at various social functions. Why do you ask?"

Forster told him. Quickly, without elaboration, he recounted the story of the Hahn family and their link to the Japanese Consulate. Ordway listened without interruption, his cigar firmly clamped between his teeth. His face was a mask when Forster finally stopped.

"In other words," he said acidly, "you've known about the situation for several days."

"Yes, sir."

"Why haven't you brought it to my attention before now?"

"I had no proof," Forster murmured. "In fact, I still don't. I only brought it up today because it's dragged on so long."

"Let me make sure I understand. You have no proof that this Morimura killed Lieutenant Tucker?"

"No, sir."

"You haven't one eyewitness who's ever seen Morimura and Dr. Hahn together?"

"No . . . not really."

"And thus far the Hahn girl has told you nothing, correct?"

"I think she will, Admiral. It's just a matter of time."

"Then why not wait until you have something solid? Why bother me with it now?"

"I was trying to make a point, sir."

"Very well, make it!"

Forster cleared his throat. "We know Susan Hahn has infiltrated every aspect of the fleet. We know her father went to some trouble to obtain aerial photographs of Pearl Harbor. And it's definite that Mrs. Hahn made at least two drops to Morimura."

"I'm still waiting to hear your point."

"Admiral, we're talking about organized espionage. These people were planted here for one purpose only."

"I assume you mean an attack on Pearl Harbor?"

"Yes, sir. Why else would the Japs have gone to all that

trouble? A German undercover agent and his family, imported to Hawaii — it wouldn't make sense otherwise."

Ordway's tone was reproachful. "On the contrary, it makes excellent sense. Japan needs up to the minute intelligence on the Pacific Fleet. We post the only threat to their plans in Southeast Asia. Why wouldn't they spy on us?"

"It's too elaborate," Forster said stubbornly. "Morimura could gather general intelligence on his own. I'm convinced we're on the same list as the Philippines and Singapore. And I think it will be soon, Admiral — damn soon."

"Well, you haven't convinced me. And at the risk of repeating myself, Washington quite obviously doesn't share your view. We would have been the first to know in that event."

Ordway checked his watch. "I'm late for lunch with Admiral Kimmel. Good work on the Hahns and Morimura. Keep me advised of developments."

"Admiral — "

"As for your Pearl Harbor theory, I suggest you go back to the drawing board."

Ordway marched from the room. Forster stood for a moment with his head bowed, thoroughly at a loss. Then he straightened and looked up at the large wall map. His eyes searched the vast emptiness of the Pacific. He thought the Jap carriers were out there, even now. And drawing ever closer.

As Forster returned to his office, Earl Bradford rushed in and extended a message form.

"Hot off the wire," Bradford said, handing it to him.

"What is it?"

"Another 'Magic' intercept from ONI."

Forster's eyes flickered over the dispatch, his attention was riveted. He started again at the beginning.

SOURCES CONSIDERED RELIABLE INDICATE TOKYO HAS INSTRUCTED MINORU TERASAKI TO DEPART FOR SOUTH AMERICA NO LATER THAN 6 DECEMBER. TERASAKI CURRENTLY SERVING AS

NAVAL ATTACHE IN WASHINGTON EMBASSY. FBI IDENTIFIES TERASAKI AS HEAD OF JAPANESE ESPIONAGE FOR WESTERN HEMISPHERE.

Forster looked up. "Why December 6?"

"Simple," Bradford replied. "He knows too much. The Japs want him out before the shooting starts."

"No, I'm talking about the date. It sounds like a deadline of some sort."

Bradford nodded. "You think they're planning to kick it off on the seventh?"

"I think you'd better keep your ear glued to radio Tokyo."

"The 'Winds' code?"

"Yeah," Forster said grimly. "I have a feeling they're going to play our song."

"Song?"

"No music, Earl, just the lyrics. East Wind Rain."

18

"Hello."
"Dr. Hahn?"
"Speaking."
"I am calling to remind you of your dental appointment."
"Of course, thank you. I will be there."
"And Dr. Hahn?"
"Yes."
"I suggest you arrange to come alone."
A beat slipped past, no more than a shallow intake of breath. "I understand."
Morimura hung up and stepped out of the phone booth. He laughed inwardly, imagining the consternation at Naval Intelligence when their agent reported he'd made an untraceable call. It seemed a fitting touch for an already extraordinary day.
He led his shadow back to the consulate.

It was almost four in the afternoon. Hahn was seated behind his desk in the study. His pipe had gone cold and his eyes were fixed on the wall clock. He watched the second hand tick onward with an empty stare.
Since returning home, he had spoken to no one. Greta was asleep and Susan was still out, and he welcomed the quiet. His thoughts turned inward, he had reviewed the situation from

every possible perspective. His resolve was now stripped of all emotion.

There was no question that the authorities would apprehend them. His whole family, Greta and Susan would eventually stand before a tribunal. As for himself, the sentence imposed would almost certainly result in his execution. He seemed to recall that in America they hang spies, which struck him as thoroughly undignified. He would have preferred a firing squad.

The alternative, which he'd rejected, was to flee Hawaii. By activating the emergency escape plan, he could spirit his family onto a passenger liner bound for the mainland. From there, via South America, his espionage contacts would arrange safe passage to Germany. But to quit and run, merely to save his family, would violate his oath to the Fatherland. He found death preferable to disgrace.

Leaning forward, Hahn turned the page on his desk calendar. The date was Saturday, December 6. For a moment, he imagined himself in command of a Japanese fleet lying off the coast of Oahu. Then, weighing all the known factors, he considered the optimum time for an attack on Pearl Harbor. He riffled the calendar pages, turned one last page, and stopped on December 7.

A Sunday. Traditionally the one day of the week when Americans lazed about, the day of rest. And a day when security gave way to the pursuit of pleasure. Some inner conviction told Hahn he need turn the calendar no further. His mission would end tomorrow.

The front door opened. From the street, there was the muffled sound of a car pulling away. Then the door closed and Susan started across the foyer. She paused in the doorway.

"Good afternoon, Papa." She smiled wistfully.

"How was Lieutenant Gordon?"

"Oh, his usual boring self. He never changes."

Susan lied with convincing ease. She had not mentioned having seen Bendix. Nor had she voiced her belief that he'd been recruited by Naval Intelligence. To do so would automatically invoke his death warrant, for her father would not hesitate to have him killed. She was reconciled to the deception, her betrayal by omission. Nothing mattered now.

"Gordon's personality," Hahn said bluntly, "does not interest me. What were you able to learn from him?"

"Very little I'm afraid. It seems no one tells submariners anything of importance."

"Are you saying you learned *nothing*?"

Her eyes fell before his gaze. "Nothing new, Papa. Just more speculation and rumors."

Hahn drummed his fingers on the desktop. "I need information on battleships and carriers. When is your next date with either Dunn or Crane?"

"I'm to see Peter Crane tonight."

"Excellent timing! Indeed, it couldn't be better. Listen closely, my dear."

"Yes, Papa."

"I must have the answers to certain questions. All are vital, absolutely vital!"

Hahn hesitated, waiting until she nodded. "You are to determine the next scheduled sailing date for the *Lexington*. Crane will undoubtedly know the operational orders for his own ship."

"Yes, I'm sure he will."

"Next," Hahn said emphatically, "you must find out why all the battleships are in port at the same time. I have to know when and if these ships are scheduled to depart Pearl Harbor."

"I'll try, Papa."

"No! You will not try. You will do it!"

"I only meant it might be difficult. Carrier pilots generally know very little about battleships."

"Then arrange to dance with Frank Dunn, or that Bendix fellow. Do I have to instruct you in the means of inducement?"

"No, Papa. I'll think of something."

"See that you do," Hahn growled. "Now, the last item, and perhaps the most important of all. Bring me every possible detail on the PBY squadrons. How many planes go out each day? What are their patrol sectors? How far out to sea do they fly?" He paused, suddenly thoughtful. "It occurs to me that Crane might be a very good source. He probably knows all the PBY pilots."

"I imagine he does."

"Good! You will remember all I have said?"

"Yes, Papa."

"Do not fail me. We have entered a critical stage in our mission. I must have this information—every detail—before midnight. Is that clear?"

"I understand perfectly, Papa."

Susan thought she'd never seen such an expression on his face. His eyes glittered and his complexion was flushed. He looked like a man on the verge of some marvelous coup. Or perhaps a conquest.

"Apart from the battleships, I have only one other interest. You must determine the location of the *Enterprise*."

"By now, she must be on her way back from Wake Island. She sailed eight days ago."

"Assume nothing. A carrier could easily be diverted and ordered onto patrol. I must know if the *Enterprise* is scheduled to arrive in port tomorrow."

"Tomorrow," Susan repeated, almost to herself. "May I ask you something, Papa?"

"Of course."

"You've never been this insistent before. What makes tomorrow so important?"

Hahn was silent so long she thought he intended to ignore the question. She saw the rings under his eyes and the waxy pallor of exhaustion on his features. Yet there was a glittery aspect in his gaze and she sensed barely constrained excitement. He reminded her of a tightly wound spring.

"I am pleased," Hahn said at length. "Your change in attitude indicates you have come to your senses. So I will tell you a secret."

"What sort of secret, Papa?"

Hahn placed his hands on his knees, shoulders squared. He

seemed to swell with sudden self-importance. "Tomorrow our work here comes to an end."

"It does?"

"Unless I am mistaken, the Japanese will attack. Everything points to Sunday as the opportune moment. And no Sunday will ever quite equal tomorrow."

Susan looked staggered. "The Japanese are going to attack Pearl Harbor?"

"You sound surprised."

"Everyone said it would be the Philippines. No one expects an attack here."

"Come now," Hahn chortled. "Why do you think we've spent years on this godforsaken island?"

"I don't—" Susan stopped, shook her head. "I thought we were just reporting on the fleet . . . in case of war."

"And so we were. With the hope, of course, that the Japanese would destroy the Pacific Fleet. I assumed you understood."

"No," Susan said in a small voice. "I had no idea."

"Then it's good we had a talk. You still have much to accomplish, and all of it vital. I want that information by the evening."

"Yes, Papa. I will remember."

Hahn abruptly stood. He looked at her a moment, then walked out the door. His footsteps faded down the stairway.

A tremor passed through Susan's body. Her vision blurred and for an instant she felt as if she would faint. Then, from somewhere inside, she summoned an unforeseen strength. She took a deep breath, composed herself. She knew what she must do.

19

THERE WERE THREE more TOP SECRET dispatches.

Forster lit a cigarette. He was already on the second pack today, and his mouth tasted like the inside of a rusty bucket. He exhaled smoke with a sharp outrush of breath.

The dispatches were fanned across his desktop. All of them had arrived within the past hour. Added to a radio intercept, which Bradford had decrypted only minutes ago, the messages made a compelling case. War was only a matter of hours away.

Forster's eyes moved from dispatch to dispatch. A CinCPAC staff conference was scheduled for 1600 and it was now half past the hour. He debated the wisdom of holding the dispatches, saying nothing to anyone until the staff conference. Only then would Admiral Kimmel hear the full story. An assessment unbiased by the naval bureaucrats in Washington. Or Ordway.

The thought triggered a painful association. From Ordway, his mind skipped momentarily to Kathryn. Last night, when she learned he was using Bendix to get at Susan, she'd walked out on him. She refused to talk with him on the phone and he'd finally stopped calling. He had no idea whether or not she'd spoken with Susan Hahn. But it was quite clear that nothing had happened to diminish her anger. At odd moments, he wondered if it was irreconcilable. Then, swamped by the flow of intelligence data, his mind was diverted from personal matters. War, not unlike an opiate, tended to be addictive.

Forster glanced at his watch. He saw that it was twenty-five minutes of four, and time to make a decision. His conscience told him to wait and present the dispatches at the staff conference. His common sense told him it would be a quixotic gesture, as well as a direct violation of orders. Last time Ordway had bluntly warned him that such actions would not be tolerated. His common sense prevailed.

Upstairs, he was ushered into Ordway's office. Captain Edward McNally, CinCPAC Operations Officer, was seated before the desk. Forster considered him something of a drone, capable but no mental giant. Like most career officers, he followed the axiom of go along to get along. He was an ardent supporter of the status quo.

"Come in, Forster." Ordway motioned him to a chair. "We were just reviewing areas to be covered at the staff meeting. Anything new on the intelligence front?"

"Yes, sir. We've received several dispatches within the last hour. I think the jigsaw has finally taken shape."

"Jigsaw?"

"The Jap war plan."

"Very well. Let's hear it."

"If I may, Admiral."

Forster walked to the large wall map. He indicated the blue of the South China Sea, then traced a line southward. "British Intelligence reports two Jap convoys. The first was sighted off the southern tip of Indochina. Present course dead ahead through the Gulf of Siam. That will put them within striking distance of Singapore by dawn tomorrow."

"And the second convoy?"

"Here." Forster rapped a spot on the map. "Off the coast of Indochina, well out to sea. Bearing south by southeast."

Ordway nodded. "The Philippines."

"Yes, sir. A slight change in course will position them off the

Philippines sometime tomorrow. Probably early afternoon."

Ordway exchanged a glance with McNally. "What do you think, Eddie?"

McNally shrugged. "Maybe, maybe not. It could be a scare tactic to get us back to the negotiating table. The Japs are great bluffers."

"No, sir," Forster said forcefully. "Not this time. According to the British, these are full-scale task forces. It's no bluff."

"What else?" Ordway interjected. "You mentioned several communiques."

Forster went on. "We intercepted a radio transmit from Tokyo. The passenger liner *Tatsuta Maru* has been ordered back to Japan. It was scheduled to dock Honolulu tomorrow afternoon."

"What's your point, Commander? So the Japs don't want to lose a potential ship. Sounds fairly routine considering the hostile situation."

"That is the point, sir. All our intelligence indicates the Japs will attack tomorrow. We've located the convoys bound for Singapore and the Philippines. The third task force, six aircraft carriers, still hasn't broken radio silence."

Ordway frowned. "And you still believe they're headed our way?"

"Yes, sir, I do," Forster said with conviction. "Everything points to a coordinated offensive, with the Pacific Fleet as their third objective. I believe those carriers are standing off Hawaii right now. I'd stake my life they'll hit us tomorrow."

Ordway looked across the desk at McNally. "How about it, Eddie? In your opinion, what are the chances of a surprise raid on Pearl?"

"None," McNally said skeptically. "If there were, Washington would have ordered the fleet to sea long before now. I think you're jumping at shadows, Forster."

Forster ignored him. "Admiral, I'd like to offer a recommendation."

"What is it," Ordway asked.

"At the moment, we only have seven PBYs operational. And they're all patrolling south by southwest."
"Are you suggesting that's inadequate?"
"Yes, sir. I recommend we put more planes in the air and extend our recon area to the north by northwest quadrant."
"Why north by northwest?"
"In all our war games, Admiral, the attacking force struck from the north. Something tells me the Japs took the lesson to heart."
"The Joint Defense Plan covers that eventuality. However, expanded patrols will not—repeat *will not*—be undertaken unless intelligence indicates a high probability of attack. You have yet to demonstrate that those carriers are anywhere near Hawaiian waters."
"Admiral, we'll never know if they're out there or not unless we take a look. All I'm suggesting is an ounce of prevention."
"Request denied. And I don't want your theories brought up during the staff meeting. Unless Admiral Kimmel addresses you directly, you're to say nothing. Do I make myself clear?"
"What about today's dispatches, sir?"
"You needn't worry, Forster. I'll cover the pertinent information in my briefing."
Ordway stood and moved around the desk. As he crossed the room, McNally fell in a pace behind. Forster followed them out the door with a downcast look. He tried to remember how the old proverb went. For it seemed fittingly apropos as they trooped along the corridor. Something about the blind leading the blind.

It was late evening. Forster pushed back from his desk, sat there a moment staring at nothing. Then he vigorously massaged his eyes, scrubbed his face with upturned palms. He felt curiously like a man who had walked into cobwebs.
Earl Bradford came through the door with steaming mugs of coffee. He was about to speak when the phone jangled a shrill ring. Forster waved him to a chair and lifted the receiver.
"Commander Forster."

"Evening, Forster. This is Lamar Moody."

"Hello, stranger. How are things with the G-men?"

"Busy." Moody sounded harassed. "You remember our conversation about phone taps?"

"Of course."

"There were several local Japanese on our list of possible subversives. One of them is a Honolulu dentist, Dr. Motokazu Mori. He got an interesting phone call about an hour ago. I'm looking at the transcript."

"Who was the call from?"

"Someone who identified himself as editor of the *Yomiuri Shinbun*. That's the morning newspaper in Tokyo."

"Tokyo!" Forster sat bolt erect.

"Thought you might be interested. Among other things, the editor asked about searchlights, the weather . . . and flowers."

"Did you say flowers?"

"Yeah. Now let me quote Mori's reply. His exact words were: 'The hibiscus and the poinsettia are in bloom.' Does that mean anything to you?"

"Not offhand," Forster said evasively. "How did the editor phrase his questions?"

"Well, first, he talked about the weather. Actually, it was a statement rather than a question. He said he'd heard wind and rain are expected in Hawaii. Then he asked which flowers are blooming now."

"Did he say anything about the direction of the wind?"

"How'd you know that?" Moody asked suspiciously.

"It's important, Lamar. Check your transcript and get it right."

There was a rustle of paper. "Okay, here it is. He said, and I'm quoting: 'I understand east wind and rain are expected in Hawaii. Is it a code?"

"Affirmative. The part about flowers was an acknowledgment. Listen closely, Lamar. What did the dentist do after the phone call?"

"His office is in the Oriental quarter below Hotel Street. He made a beeline from there to the Japanese consulate."

"Damn!"

"All right, Forster, let's level. What's going on?"

"Get yourself a helmet, Lamar."

"Wait a—"

Forster hung up. His gaze fixed on Bradford. "Do you have anyone monitoring shortwave broadcasts tonight?"

Bradford nodded. "All we're getting is static. There's some sort of atmospheric interference."

"Clever bastards. No radio, so they used a transpacific phone call."

"The 'Winds' execute?"

"Loud and clear, Earl. Word for word."

Forster rose and hurried from the room. As he went out the door, the phone began ringing. Bradford waited until he was gone before answering. Lamar Moody was still cursing.

Forster walked straight through the lobby of the Halekulani Hotel. On the oceanside, overlooking Waikiki Beach, he turned toward a broad terrace. A dinner party was underway beneath the bowers of a massive hau tree.

The host and hostess were Admiral and Mrs. Fairfax Leary. The guest of honor was Admiral H. E. Kimmel. Among the other officers present were Ordway and McNally. They spotted Forster at almost the exact moment.

Ordway quickly excused himself. He rose from the table and proceeded at a rapid pace along the terrace. He intercepted Forster some distance from the dinner party. His voice was terse.

"What's the meaning of this?"

"I have to see Admiral Kimmel," Forster said firmly. "Now."

"I'll have an explanation, Forster. And by God it better be good!"

"We received the 'Winds' execute tonight."

" 'Winds' execute? What are you talking about?"

"East wind rain," Forster told him. "The alert advising imminent hostilities between the United States and Japan. It was delivered to the Japanese consulate not quite two hours ago."

"How do you mean, delivered?"

Forster briefly related the details. Ordway listened without expression, staring out to sea. When Forster stopped, he slowly shook his head. "It sounds too pat. Have you actually seen this transcript yourself?"

"No, sir."

"Then get a copy. And arrange for a copy of the original Japanese. I want our own translators to go over it carefully."

"Admiral, that would take most of the night."

"Just do it," Ordway replied sharply. "Have it ready for me first thing in the morning. If it's genuine, I'll act on it at that time."

Forster started around him. "Tomorrow's too late. Admiral Kimmel has to be advised now."

"*Hear me*," Ordway commanded. "I just gave you a direct order. Follow it or I'll have you placed under house arrest."

"How would you explain that to Admiral Kimmel?"

"How would you explain this so-called 'Winds' execute? The admiral would ask for proof positive—exactly as I've done."

Forster stared at him with cold contempt. "I'll have the translation in your office by midnight. If you're not there, I'll take it to Admiral Kimmel's home."

"Don't press your luck, mister. I'm warning—"

"Midnight. Be there or not, suit yourself. I won't wait."

Forster walked off into the night.

20

OFFICERS AND THEIR ladies mobbed the dance floor at the Officers' Club. There was standing room only at the bar and every table was either occupied or reserved. The overflow crowd was attributed to a first for the Pacific Fleet. No one could recall all the battleships at anchor on a weekend.

Around eight, Susan arrived on Peter Crane's arm. Hardly anyone missed her entrance, for she put on an especially bold front tonight. She wore an elegant silver brocade blouse with puffed sleeves and scoop-necked decolletage. Her evening skirt was sleek black velvet, banded at the waist to emphasize her figure. She looked like an animated voluptuary, all grace and motion. Her smile was luminous.

Crane had reserved a small table near the orchestra. Their waiter took drink orders and left them with menus. While Crane studied the selection, Susan looked airily around the room. She saw nothing of Kathryn and Forster, and their absence came as a distinct relief. For all her vibrant manner, she simply couldn't have contended with them tonight. There were too many other worries, too little time. One night to accomplish so much.

The past few days had been a total nightmare. Susan shared her father's sense of desperation. She had no idea whether he was aware of Forster's investigation, and she wasn't about to ask. But she was quite certain they would be arrested sometime tomorrow. Once the Japanese attacked, there would be no reason for Forster to delay further. Still, what happened to her and her family was now almost incidental. She somehow thought it predestined that they would never return to Germany.

Tonight, her concern centered solely on Harry Bendix. She had left a phone message at the Officers' Mess, asking him to meet her at the club. After what had happened, she knew he had every right to despise and loathe her. Yet she prayed that he still loved her. For she was prepared to beguile and deceive, to trade on their love one last time. She was determined that he would not return to his ship tonight. Or tomorrow.

After dinner, Frank Dunn stopped by the table. He asked her to dance and she stilled Crane's objection with a pat on the cheek. Only when they were on the dance floor did she realize that she was even now playing the role. If tonight went as planned, she would not return home. Nor would she see her father before tomorrow.

By then the information would be valueless. But she was in Dunn's arms and she saw no reason not to ask. He told her none of the battleships would sail before the middle of the week. To her next inquiry, he remarked that the *Enterprise* had been delayed by rough weather. According to scuttlebutt, the carrier would return to port on Monday.

Dunn kept her on the dance floor through a medley. When he saw her back to the table, Crane was visibly annoyed. She laughed and playfully pinched his leg under the table. Still iron-jawed, Crane tried to stifle a smile. His eyes gave him away.

"You're a real pill. You enjoy making us suffer, don't you?"

"Who?" Susan teased.

"Who, my foot!" Crane scoffed. "You know damn well who. Dunn and me and all the others, that's who!"

"What a dreadful thing to say. You make me sound like a — coquette."

"If the shoe fits, wear it."

"Why, Peter Crane!"

"C'mon, 'fess up. You're a born flirt! You enjoy it."

"If you think that, why do you even bother? I'm sure you know lots of girls."

"No," Crane said, suddenly serious. "None like you. I shouldn't say it, but you're in a league by yourself. I guess that's why we hang around."

"We?"

"Your admirers. Susie Hahn's legion."

"Legion indeed! Now you make me sound like the Pied Piper."

Crane smiled broadly, rolled his eyes. "You do play a wicked flute. And I'm not talking woodwinds . . . if you get my meaning."

Susan laughed with him. "I think you're terrible."

"No, you don't. If anything, you're flattered!"

Susan put on a mock pout. But inside, she knew he'd spoken the truth. She was proud of her power over men. Even now, with the world falling apart around her, she couldn't resist playing the femme fatale. She thought that it had become almost second nature, an automatic reflex. Or perhaps Peter Crane was wiser than even he suspected. Perhaps she'd been born to the role.

Inwardly troubled, her gaze drifted out across the crowd. Their gaiety and laughter, their time of innocence, would soon vanish forever. She wondered how tomorrow would alter their lives, their naiveté and their insular outlook. Then, quite suddenly, a wayward doubt flitted through her mind. Perhaps it wouldn't happen.

She considered the possibility that her father was wrong. When Hitler balked at the English Channel, would the Japanese arrogantly cross thousands of miles of water? Would they dare challenge the Pacific Fleet so far from their homeland? To believe that one had to believe that the Americans were military dullards, incompetents. For all of them, even after the war alert, remained convinced the Japanese would attack the Philippines. Were so many wrong . . . and her father right?

She struggled with the thought a moment. No matter how much she abhorred his personal insensitivity, her father's intellect was unquestionable. He was a brilliant man, with a keen analytical mind. If he believed the Japanese were going to attack Pearl Harbor, then she could not prudently discount it. She had to assume the Americans, not her father, were wrong. And she had to reconcile herself to tomorrow, to the inevitable. What would happen would happen.

Pearl Harbor, the Pacific Fleet, none of that was her responsibility. But one man, the man who had shown her tenderness and love, was her responsibility. Harry Bendix must not die.

Crane took her hand. "Hey, wake up and join the party. You look a million miles away."

"Oh, sorry, I was just—"

She stopped, her eyes suddenly round. Across the room she saw Bendix pause in the doorway. His gaze slowly circled the tables until he found her. She nodded imperceptibly, then glanced back at Crane. Her voice turned guileless.

"Will you excuse me a minute, Peter?"

"What's wrong?"

"Nothing. I have to have a word with Kathryn, that's all."

"Kathryn?" Crane peered into the crowd. "Where is she?"

"I saw her just now, on the veranda. I won't be long."

Susan squeezed his hand, then stood. She skirted the dance floor, rapidly made her way outside. On the veranda, several couples were staring dreamily across the harbor. The water shimmered with moonbeams and lights from the fleet winked like distant fireflies. She walked to the end of the veranda, halted in a patch of shadow. A moment later Bendix joined her.

"I got your message."

"You're so late. I began to worry you wouldn't come."

"It's only a little after ten."

"Well, no matter," she said softly. "You're here now."

"Aren't you afraid your date will object?"

His injured tone shook her. "Please don't be angry. I've avoided you because I had to. Not by choice."

"Okay, forget it. What's so important? Why the sudden yen to see me?"

"I've been doing a lot of thinking. About us and the situation . . . and everything."

"I'm not sure I follow you."

"If I sound confused it's because I am. I'm still not certain I can go through with it."

"With what?"

"I . . ." she hesitated, then rushed on. "All right, I'll just ask you. Is John Forster's offer still good?"

"The amnesty?"

"Yes."

Surprise echoed in his voice. "Are you serious?"

"I think so."

"What made you change your mind?"

"You," she said simply. "I was forced to choose between you and my family. I chose you."

Bendix took her by the shoulders. "You'd do that for me?"

"Not with any peace of mind. But I will do it—on one condition."

"Condition?"

"I want us to have one last night together. Before it becomes public and the scandal starts."

"Are you talking about tonight?"

She nodded. "We can go to the windward side. I just want you to hold me and love me. It's not too much to ask, and one more night won't matter to John. I'll turn myself in to him tomorrow."

"Damn," Bendix muttered. "I can't, not tonight. I've got the midwatch."

"You mean you're on duty?"

"Midnight to eight. And no way out of it. All the senior officers are ashore for the weekend."

"There must be a way," she said frantically. "You have to find a way, Harry. You must!"

"I'm stuck. Nobody would swap watches this late."

"Please," she whispered, desperation in her voice. "I won't

have the courage another time. We have to do it tonight."

"Look, calm down. I'll be relieved at eight and we can leave then. We'll spend tomorrow and tomorrow night on the windward side. Monday morning is soon enough for Forster anyway."

Her heart sank. She debated telling him the truth, quickly discarded the idea. Even the hint of an impending attack would spoil everything. His courage, his sense of honor would never allow him to desert his ship in a moment of peril. So she had no choice but to accept, and hope the Japanese wouldn't attack too early. Her voice was strained.

"What time could you leave the ship?"

"I told you. Eight or shortly after, when I'm relieved."

"Promise you won't wait around. The minute you're off duty, just get in your car and drive straight to the house. Promise?"

"Why?" Bendix said, mystified. "What's the rush? You make it sound like life or death."

She improvised a half-truth. "I hadn't planned to go home tonight. I'll have to sneak out of the house in the morning . . . before my father awakes."

"All right, tell you what. I'll be there by eight-fifteen, eight-twenty at the latest. You just be waiting outside, ready to go."

"I will, darling. I swear I will."

She stepped into his arms. Her mouth sought his and she kissed him with fierce urgency, wanting him more at that moment than ever before. When at last they separated, a strange inner look came over her face. Her eyes blurred with tears.

"You won't let anything stop you?"

"Don't worry, I'll be there. I promise."

She choked back the tears, unable to speak. Then she kissed him and walked quickly away. At the door, some black premonition caused her to stop, look at him one last time. She smiled bravely.

Her heart told her tomorrow would never come.

Forster emerged from CinCPAC headquarters. His nerves were

jangled by too much coffee, and he'd decided he needed a drink. He turned in the direction of the club.

The waiting seemed to him interminable. Earlier, talking with Lamar Moody, he had learned that the 'Winds' phone conversation was on a wire recording. The FBI translators had worked directly from the recording, transposing it into English. There was no transcript of the original Japanese.

Earl Bradford was even now at the downtown FBI office. His orders were to reproduce, in Japanese, a written version of the recording. Only then could a direct comparison be made with the English transcript. But it was already approaching eleven, and transposing conversational idiom into Japanese characters was a laborious process. Bradford wouldn't finish before one, perhaps later.

A few minutes ago, Forster had called Ordway at home. Their meeting, he'd explained, would necessarily be delayed. Once the transcripts were in his possession, he would hand deliver them to Ordway. Upon hanging up, he's sat there staring at the second hand on his watch. He tried not to think of the Jap aircraft carriers, or the timetable for their attack. Yet he could think of nothing else.

The eleven o'clock launch pulled into Merry Point. As he approached the landing, Forster saw Harry Bendix hurrying down the path from the club. He thought Bendix looked like a man with a great deal on his mind, none of it pleasant. An instant later Bendix spotted him and appeared to break stride. Forster greeted him without expression.

"Evening, Harry."

"Commander."

"You're packing it in early tonight."

"I pulled the midwatch."

"Lucky you. How are things at the club?"

Bendix shuffled uncomfortably. "Susan's there. We just had a talk, and I'd suggest you steer clear of her. You might be one straw too many tonight."

Foster was instantly alert. "What happened?"

In a halting voice, Bendix related his conversation with Susan. Forster let him talk, listening quietly until he concluded. There was a moment of stark silence.

"Odd, isn't it?" Forster remarked. "How she was so insistent about tonight?"

"She just wants to get away from her father."

"She could have done that last night, or the night before. Why tonight?"

"What difference does it make?"

"Quite a bit, I'd say. She apparently has some reason for wanting you off the *Nevada*."

"Where'd you get that idea?"

"When you ruled out tonight, she immediately jumped on tomorrow. She made you promise to leave ship the minute you're relieved. Why so insistent?"

"I told you — her father."

"Or maybe she knows something we don't."

"About what?"

"Hard to say. But she sure wants you off that ship — and away from Pearl."

"You're talking riddles."

"I'm talking about human weakness, Harry. I think Susan just proved she has a soft spot."

"Think what you want," Bendix said, tight-lipped. "I intend to keep the date. She wants it that way, and I gave her my word. I'll bring her to you Monday morning — not before."

Forster was silent for a long moment. "What the hell? I suppose I can wait one more day."

"And you'll keep your word, too? Her testimony for a full amnesty. No monkey business?"

"A deal's a deal," Forster said equably. "You deliver and I'll deliver. Quid pro quo."

Bendix looked on the verge of saying something more. Then he nodded and walked down the path to the landing. He hopped aboard the launch, joining several officers gathered amidships. The coxswain immediately ordered the lines cast off.

Forster watched until the launch was out of sight. After a moment's reflection, he decided to take Bendix's advice. There was nothing to be gained in confronting the girl at the club. He turned back in the direction of CinCPAC headquarters.

On balance, he thought Susan's behavior had confirmed his theory about Pearl Harbor. Yet, however inadvertently, she had proved still another piece of the jigsaw. She apparently *knew* the Japs were not planning a dawn attack. Quite probably she'd been briefed by her father on the details of the raid. Otherwise she would never have allowed Bendix to remain aboard the *Nevada*.

No other reference seemed reasonable to Forster. Her every effort, clearly, was to remove Bendix from harm's way. And her actions tonight effectively ruled out an early morning strike. Whether the attack was planned for late morning, or even Sunday afternoon, was a moot point. The critical factor was one of time.

By Forster's reckoning, a lovers' tryst had granted him a reprieve. The margin, while measured in hours, was nonetheless welcome, and badly needed. With it, he might still overcome Ordway's stubborn skepticism. And convince Admiral Kimmel to act. His stride quickened. He suddenly no longer needed a drink.

21

THE ORCHESTRA PLAYED "Good Night Sweetheart." There was a collective groan from the crowd. With midnight approaching, the number signaled an end to the evening's festivities. As the last note faded, the house lights brightened in a sobering blaze. Officers and their ladies began filing slowly out of the club.

Susan pleaded a splitting headache. When Crane protested, she put him off with promises of another night. They drove from the base to Halawa Heights in a tight cone of silence. She allowed him a quick goodnight kiss, then slipped from the car, and hurried inside the house.

A light was on in the study. She closed the front door, steeling herself to face the next few minutes. Her mind was on tomorrow morning, when she must somehow sneak out of the house. But for now, she warned herself to appear normal. Her father expected a report and she dared not permit anything to arouse his suspicion. She forced herself to smile.

Hahn looked up as she entered. His eyes were bloodshot, rimmed with fatigue. Yet his expression was alert, curiously eager. "Well," he demanded. "What did you learn?"

"Everything you asked for, Papa."

"The battleships?"

"None of them will sail until sometime next week."

"Are you certain, absolutely certain?"

"Yes, Papa. I spoke with Frank Dunn, and there's no question. All the ships will remain in port."

"And the *Enterprise?*"

"On her way back from Wake Island. However, she has been delayed by bad weather. They now expect her to arrive on Monday."

"Is the information reliable?"

"I believe so, Papa. Dunn attributed it to scuttlebutt, and these rumors generally have some basis in fact. At least, that's always been true in the past."

"So," Hahn said with studied calm, "the fleet disposition will not change on Sunday." His gaze shifted to the wall clock. "Or to be more precise—today."

"Yes," Susan said softly. "Today."

"Excellent! You have performed very well indeed. I couldn't be more pleased."

"May I ask you something, Papa?"

"Of course."

"When will the Japanese attack?"

"Today. I told you that before."

"Yes, but when—what time?"

"Why do you want to know?"

"Why?" Susan repeated blankly. "Curiosity, I suppose. We've worked so long and now it ends."

Hahn stared at her. His eyes were abruptly wary, his expression guarded. He thought it unwise to tell her everything. A breach of security, even with dawn only hours away, was still possible. So he told her a lie.

"Our friend at the consulate estimates somewhere between eleven o'clock and noon. Church services are held during those hours, and it's the perfect time for an attack. I suspect the Americans will be taken completely by surprise."

"Yes, I'm sure they will, Papa."

"If there's nothing else—" Hahn got to his feet. "I must be on my way now. Our friend expects me by one o'clock at the latest."

Susan waited in the foyer until he let himself out the door.

When she heard the car motor start, she turned and slowly mounted the stairs. Her thoughts leaped ahead to the morning, calculating time and distance. Even if Harry were delayed, she realized, there was an hour or more to spare. Her heart was suddenly lighter.

By eleven o'clock, they would be on the windward side. It occurred to her that her father might be lying. But then, she asked herself what purpose a lie would serve. There seemed no logical reason, and besides, an attack during church services made excellent sense. She decided he'd told her the truth.

Hahn used evasive tactics. From Iolani Palace, where he parked the car, he walked to Hotel Street. Then he turned north, away from the Oriental quarter. He knew he was being tailed probably by a team of agents, at least three or four operatives. Still, by constantly twisting and doubling back on himself, he was satisfied he'd managed to lose them in the labyrinth of darkened sidestreets.

A few minutes before one, he crossed Hotel Street, walking south. He was unaware that no one had tailed him since he'd parked the car. Instead, playing a hunch, Lieutenant Joe Michaels had posted an agent on every corner along Hotel Street. The men were attired in slacks and aloha shirts, indistinguishable from the thousands of servicemen thronging the red-light district. One of them spotted him now and stealthily trailed him to the Oriental quarter. After Hahn entered the office building, the agent waited until he was certain it wasn't a ruse. Then he rushed off to find Joe Michaels.

Upstairs, Hahn was admitted by Morimura. Without being asked, he took a seat in the dentist's chair. Not a word was spoken while Morimura closed and locked the door. Hahn crossed his legs, watching with a rather smug look. Morimura glanced around at him.

"You seem quite pleased with yourself, Dr. Hahn. I assume the news must be good."

"Far better than you could imagine."

"Well?"

"All eight battleships will remain in port."

"For how long?"

"Please." Hahn motioned with a disdainful hand. "We both know the attack is only hours away. Why pretend tomorrow or the next day has any relevance?"

Morimura ignored the question. "How dependable is your source?"

"Communications Officer on the *Arizona*. I daresay we can accept it at face value."

"How current is the information?"

Hahn checked his watch. "To be precise, forty-nine minutes. Would you say that is timely enough?"

The patronizing tone stung. Morimura glowered at him a moment, then nodded. "What can you tell me about the *Enterprise*?"

"Delayed by rough seas. A pity, but she won't arrive until tomorrow. Your bombers will lose the chance to sink a carrier."

"You sound very confident. How do we know the *Enterprise* hasn't been ordered on patrol?"

"We know because my daughter reports it so. I think that should prove entirely adequate,.even for you."

"You seem intent on insulting me, Dr. Hahn. May I inquire why?"

Hahn laughed harshly. "We shan't see each other again after tonight. I wouldn't want to end our association on a cordial note. Unlike you, I'm no hypocrite."

Morimura's expression was unreadable. He overlooked the affront, focusing instead on the situation. The "Winds" code alert, which he'd received earlier, simplified things greatly. By sunrise, or shortly thereafter, the attack on Pearl Harbor would commence. So tonight's meeting was indeed his last with Eric Hahn. He no longer needed the German.

"Have you anything else to report?"

"No," Hahn replied. "I believe that concludes our business."

"Not quite."

Morimura's eyes suddenly turned cold. He stood, pulling the switchblade from his pocket, and pressed the release button. The blade sprang open, glinting dully in the lamplight. Hahn reacted in the same instant. His hand dipped inside his suit jacket and reappeared with a Walther automatic. He wagged the snout of the pistol.

"Drop it."

The knife clattered to the floor.

"Sit down."

Morimura looked surprised. He gingerly lowered himself into the desk chair. Hahn smiled distantly, as though at some private joke. Then he got to his feet.

"I really should kill you. Believe me, nothing would give me greater pleasure."

"What stops you?"

"Unfortunately, you are not expendable. Not tonight at any rate."

"Are you referring to your report?"

Hahn nodded. "I trust you will radio Tokyo immediately. The carrier force must have that information before launching the attack." He paused for effect. "It is the only reason I spare your life."

"If you will, permit me a question. How did you know I meant to kill you?"

"You are Japanese."

"I beg your pardon?"

"No sane man would trust an Oriental. You are a very treacherous people."

"And the Germans are not?"

Hahn unlocked the door. "There is an essential difference. We kill only our enemies — never our friends."

Morimura sniffed. "You are hardly a friend."

"I am reminded again that it is difficult to mock a fool." Hahn grinned. *"Sayonara."*

The door opened and closed. Hahn's footsteps faded along the hallway. His laugh lingered behind.

It was two o'clock in the morning.

Forster's eyes felt gritty. His head pounded, and a pulse throbbed at his temple. On the desktop before him were transcripts of the "Winds" code phone conversation. One was in handwritten Japanese characters and the other had been translated into English. He read through the English version with meticulous care.

Earl Bradford had returned shortly before the hour. Transcribing the FBI wire recording, which proved to be of poor quality, had taken him far longer than anticipated. After delivering the transcripts, he'd been summoned almost immediately to the communications room. And now, as Forster turned the last page, Bradford hurried back into the office. He looked worried.

"Helluva job, Earl," Forster congratulated him. "Even Ordway will have to admit it's the 'Winds' alert."

"We've got another problem. Our radio intercept picked up a transmission from the Jap consulate. They're sending fast and heavy."

"Any chance you can read it?"

Bradford shook his head. "It's a code we've never heard before. Probably their last-ditch emergency cipher."

"What's your best guess?"

The phone rang. Forster motioned Bradford to a chair, then lifted the receiver. "Commander Forster."

"Joe Michaels, sir."

"What's up, Joe?"

"Hahn and Morimura. They definitely met tonight. No mistake about it."

"How do you know?"

"I suckered Hahn into thinking he'd lost us. One of my men tailed him to an office building in the Oriental quarter."

"Was there a Jap dentist's office in the building?"

'Yes, sir, there was. How'd you know that?"

"Never mind." Forster said briskly. "Just tell me what happened. Take it from the top."

"Well, the Hahn girl got home a little after midnight. A few minutes later the old man took off like a ruptured goose. We trailed him downtown, then to the office building."

"Go on."

"He stayed inside about twenty minutes. When he came out, I put two men on him and they followed him back home. He's there now."

"And Morimura?"

"He came out ten minutes or so after Hahn. I tailed him myself, back to the consulate."

"Where was the team assigned to Morimura?"

"They never knew he was gone. But don't fault them, Commander. I saw him scale the back wall on his way into the consulate. That's probably the way he got out."

Forster was silent a moment. "What time did Morimura return to the consulate?"

"O-one-thirty on the nose."

"Thanks, Joe. Keep your boys on stakeout. We're in for a busy night."

Forster hung up. He looked across the desk at Bradford. "What time did the consulate start transmitting?"

"O-one-fifty-five."

"It all fits. Morimura met with Hahn about one. Then he hotfooted it back to the consulate and started encoding. That's what we're hearing now."

"A final report on the fleet?"

"Very final, Earl. One last update before the shooting starts."

Forster stuffed the transcripts into a large manila envelope. He rose and moved around the desk. Bradford scrambled to his feet.

"Where are you going?"

"Ordway's home. It's showdown time."

Forster stalked out of the office.

22

THERE WAS NO traffic on Kamehameha Road. Once through the main gate, Forster put the gas pedal on the floorboard and held it there. He drove like a man possessed.

Until now, he'd formulated no definite plan. But Joe Michael's phone call put an altogether different light on the situation. As of tonight, there was conclusive proof linking the Hahn family to Morimura and the Japanese consulate. All the more important, proof of an entrenched espionage ring buttressed his central argument. The "Winds" code alert was a legitimate war signal.

Yet, for all the proof, one critical unknown still remained. Ordway was inflexible, almost immovable, once he'd taken a position. Whether or not he would admit his mistake was open to question. Somehow, though, he had to be persuaded that the fleet was in imminent peril. Unless he agreed to alert Admiral Kimmel, then only one alternative existed. Ordway would have to be bypassed—tonight.

A stray thought suddenly struck Forster. The memory of the fight with Kathryn was all too vivid, and painful. Over the past twenty-four hours he'd been so absorbed by the threat to Pearl Harbor that every waking moment was devoted to the missing Jap carriers. But now, speeding toward the Ordway home, it occurred to him that he might see Kathryn. He wondered what they would say to one another. He wondered if there was anything left to say.

All their differences, including her concern for his career, were invariably linked to her father. So their estrangement went deeper than her normal outrage over Susan. The root cause was a father who tyrannically dictated values, and a daughter who submitted with only token resistance. Kathryn was not yet her own person, a self-sufficient individual. She was, instead, Admiral Thomas Ordway's daughter. A grown woman who still thought like a girl.

Forster was not optimistic. His resentment was tempered by loving remembrances of all they'd shared. But love without commitment seemed to him doomed to fall apart like an empty affair. And he doubted now that Kathryn would ever commit herself. She simply wasn't strong enough to make the break with her father. Or perhaps she just didn't care enough. In his mind, it all amounted to the same thing.

A mile or so from the base he turned off the main road. The Makalapa district, where Ordway lived, was an exclusive neighborhood with rambling homes and spacious lawns. As he rounded the corner onto Samoa Place, it occurred to him that he'd forgotten to call Ordway. But on second thought, he realized he hadn't really forgotten. The decision to appear unannounced, however unwittingly made, was nonetheless deliberate. Ordway could hardly turn him away.

The house was dark. Forster parked at the curb and killed the engine. With the manila envelope under his arm, he proceeded up the walkway. He halted on the porch and gave the doorbell three sharp blasts. In rapid succession, he gave it three more and still another three. A light appeared at the back of the house, and moments later someone switched on the vestibule chandelier. Ordway threw open the door.

"Forster!"

"Good morning, Admiral."

"What time is it?"

"Not quite three."

"What the hell do—"

Forster held up the envelope. "May I come in, Admiral? I have the information you requested."

"The 'Winds' code?"

"Yes, sir."

"You might have had the decency to call first."

"Things have been a little hectic, sir. I forgot."

"All right, step inside."

Forster moved past him into the vestibule. Ordway stumped through the door to the living room, switching on an overhead light. He wore pajamas and robe, and a pair of dog-eared slippers. His hair was mussed, and sleep gummed his eyes. He sat down heavily on the couch.

"Let's get to it. What do you have to show me?"

Forster took a chair opposite him. Opening the envelope, he pulled out the transcripts and placed them side by side on the coffee table. He tapped one, then the other.

"Original Japanese and an English translation. Earl Bradford copied it directly off the FBI recording."

Ordway scowled down at the transcripts. "How do I know he got it right? I don't read Japanese."

"I do," Forster said evenly. "And I took the time to check his translation. It's word for word, Admiral."

"Hello, John."

Kathryn appeared in the doorway. Her hair was freshly brushed and she wore a light wrapper over her nightgown. Oddly, her face looked ravaged, like someone in deep mourning. Her smile was tentative.

Forster rose. "Sorry to disturb you, Kathryn. It couldn't wait."

"I heard you mention the Japanese."

"Yes, that's right. We've come into possession of certain . . . documents."

"Oh." Her voice was flat and toneless. "Shall I make coffee, Daddy?"

"Please," Ordway grunted. "I need something to open my eyes."

Kathryn avoided Forster's gaze. She turned and disappeared down the hall. Ordway massaged his face roughly, ran a hand through his hair. Then he leaned forward and picked up the English transcript. He began reading as Forster once more sat down.

A short while later Kathryn returned with a serving tray. She placed cups and saucers on the table, and poured from a steaming coffee pot. With a quick glance at Forster, she took a seat on the couch. They sipped in silence, the only sound the rustle of paper as Ordway plowed through the transcript. He finally turned the last page.

"It's somewhat ambiguous," he said, looking up at Forster. "However, the key words are all there. It could be the 'Winds' code alert."

"Admiral, several things have happened tonight. All of them substantiate what I said earlier. That phone conversation is a war signal, straight from Tokyo."

"Are you saying you have supporting material?"

"Yes, sir."

"Then get to it! How can I make a determination without all the facts?"

Forster quickly recounted the evening's events. He began with the meeting between Hahn and Morimura. Then, emphasizing the time element, he told of the heavy radio traffic from the Japanese consulate. He concluded on a sobering note.

"All of it meshes perfectly. The 'Winds' alert, the meeting, and now a rush to get off one last report. We're about to be attacked, Admiral."

Ordway appeared dubious. "I agree, if you're talking about the Philippines. I've yet to be convinced about Pearl Harbor."

"Frankly, sir, I'm not surprised. So I held back a trump card, just to make the point."

"What do you mean, trump card?"

"Susan Hahn accepted my offer of amnesty."

"*What?*" Kathryn gasped.

Her shoulders slumped and tears welled up in her eyes. Forster stared at her a moment before looking back at Ordway. His voice measured, he related Susan's arrangement with Harry Bendix. His stress was on the time factor.

"Her one concern," he observed, "is to get Bendix off the *Nevada*. She knows the Japs are going to attack and she doesn't want him killed. There's no other explanation."

A strained stillness fell over the room. Kathryn dug a tissue out of her pocket and blew her nose. Comprehension and a dulled look of resignation were etched on her features. Ordway was silent for a time, thoughtful. At last, almost reluctantly, he nodded.

"Very well. I'll bring all this to Admiral Kimmel's attention first thing in the morning."

"No, sir," Forster said bluntly. "It has to be done now."

"Why now?"

"The fleet has to put to sea, Admiral. And that takes time, several hours. We can't afford delay."

"Look here, Forster. I'm still not fully convinced. But even if I were, the Hahn girl's actions preclude an early morning attack. You just said so yourself."

"I'm only guessing. It's possible I misread her. Or maybe she doesn't actually know the Jap timetable. The point is, we can't risk it, Admiral. We must get those ships out of the harbor!"

"Listen to yourself," Ordway scoffed. "Every other word is a *guess* or a *maybe*. I can't run to Kimmel with nothing but supposition."

"Well, I can," Forster informed him. "And if you don't, I damn sure will."

Ordway's voice rose angrily. "That's it! Consider yourself under arrest, mister. I warned you I wouldn't tolerate further insubordination."

"Stop it!" Kathryn shouted, suddenly jumping to her feet. "Why must you always be at one another's throats? Surely there's a way besides this — a compromise."

"Compromise?" Ordway repeated the word as though it were foreign to his tongue. "I believe we're past the point of compromise."

"Daddy, please, don't be such a fool. You sound incredibly pompous."

"Young lady, I will not—"

She turned to Forster. "John, you said Susan was willing to cooperate. Suppose you speeded it up somehow?"

"I don't follow you."

"If you're so certain, why not go ahead and take her into custody? Wouldn't her confession corroborate everything you've said?"

"Yeah, assuming she would talk."

"She will if it means saving Harry Bendix. Apparently that's the *only* thing on her mind right now."

"It might work," Forster said slowly. "Of course, I'd have to arrest the whole family. We couldn't risk letting Hahn get word to Morimura." He paused, considering. "And then there's the matter of time. We're already pressing our luck."

"The alternative," Kathryn insisted, "seems to be your own arrest. What would that accomplish?"

"Nothing," Forster admitted. "I'll have to move quickly, though. And I'll need authority of some sort, they're civilians."

"What about your FBI friend?"

"Not a chance . . . unless the request came from someone too high to ignore."

Kathryn fixed her father with a look. "Well, Daddy? Don't just sit there. Say something!"

Ordway reddened, his features set in a bulldog scowl. His gaze quickly shifted to Forster. "Who is the agent in charge?"

"Lamar Moody. He's been in on the case from the beginning."

"Very well. I'll call him and request his assistance. Keep me advised of developments. No more surprises!"

"Aye, aye, sir."

Kathryn walked Forster to the door. He motioned her outside, and she followed him onto the porch. They stood a moment, bathed in moonlight, awkwardly searching for words. He cleared his throat of a sudden tightness.

"I don't know if it's the right thing to say"—his shoulders lifted in a shrug—"but that wasn't daddy's little girl talking just now. I'm damn proud of you, Kate."

Her eyes were shining moistly. "You know something, sailor? I'm sort of proud of myself."

"Well, I knew all along—"

"Wait," she said, stopping him. "I'm also very ashamed of myself. I was wrong about you and everything else, especially Susan. I put you through misery and . . . "

Her voice trailed off and a teardrop rolled down her cheek. Forster scooped her into his arms, kissed her long and hard on the mouth. There was a faint saltiness on her lips, and when he released her she brushed away the tears with the back of her mind. Her voice was husky.

"Do me a favor?"

"Name it."

"Make an honest woman of me."

Forster laughed deeply in his chest. He tilted her chin up and kissed her eyes, then her mouth. It was all the answer she needed, and neither of them spoke. She waited there as Forster hurried down the walkway to his car. He drove off toward Pearl Harbor.

23

DAWN SLOWLY SWEPT the darkened sky. The Pearl Harbor Striking Force stood some two hundred miles northwest of Oahu. As the sky brightened, signal flags aboard the *Akagi* were hoisted to half-mast. The signal was a standby order, alerting the fleet to prepare for launch. The six carriers swung hard aport into an easterly wind.

Admiral Chuichi Nagumo observed from the bridge of the *Akagi*. Choppy seas prevailed and his eyes narrowed as the carrier dipped into a roiling trough. Waves hammered the bow, and wind-driven, salt spray geysered skyward with explosive force. A safe launch was impossible in such seas, and he worried that planes would be lost. But then he told himself what he'd told his staff only an hour before. There was no turning back now.

On the flight deck below, pilots revved the motors of their planes. They wore the ceremonial *hashamaki*, a white headband which symbolized their willingness to die for the Emperor. The noise was deafening, and the cheers of officers and crewmen gathered amidships were drowned out as the engines wound higher. A pall of blue exhaust smoke drifted leeward, toward the stern.

Admiral Kusaka appeared on the bridge. His duties as Chief of Staff were unrelenting, and this morning his features were particularly somber. Halting, he waited until Nagumo looked around, then nodded his head in a respectful bow. He extended a message form.

"From Tokyo, Admiral. A final intelligence report."

Nagumo unfolded the slip of paper. He turned out of the wind, bracing himself against the roll of the ship. His eyes skipped rapidly over the words.

ON THE EVENING OF DECEMBER 6 THE FOLLOWING SHIPS WERE AT ANCHOR IN PEARL HARBOR: 8 BATTLESHIPS, 3 HEAVY CRUISERS, 4 LIGHT CRUISERS, 29 DESTROYERS AND 5 SUBMARINES. HONOLULU REPORTS NONE OF THE BATTLESHIPS ARE SCHEDULED TO SAIL ON DECEMBER 7. THE CARRIER ENTERPRISE DELAYED BY HEAVY SEAS. ESTIMATED TO ARRIVE PEARL HARBOR ON DECEMBER 8.

Nagumo read it through a second time. Then he folded the message form, scoring the crease with his thumbnail, and looked up. His expression was troubled.

"How do you assess the situation?"

"Favorable," Kusaka said succinctly. "An opportunity to destroy all their battleships in one blow. We could hardly ask for more."

Nagumo shook his head. "An opportunity that still bothers me. Such good fortune seems somehow suspect."

"I share your concern, Admiral. However, our agents in Honolulu have provided a reasonable explanation. We know why all the battleships are in port at the same time."

"And the carriers? Do we accept that explanation as well?"

"You refer to the *Enterprise* being delayed?"

"I do indeed," Nagumo replied. "Once we launch our planes, we will be stripped of air cover. Vulnerable to air attack."

"Yes, but consider, Admiral. What you say implies a design on the part of the Americans. I do not believe they are that clever."

"I only know that two aircraft carriers are unaccounted for. Perhaps they are returning to port and perhaps they are not. Consider what would happen if the *Enterprise* and the *Lexington* have been ordered on patrol and discover our location."

"All the information at hand is against such an eventuality."

"What information?"

"We have an English-speaking operator monitoring the civilian radio stations in Honolulu. The tone of the broadcasts seems quite normal, weather reports and music."

"Hardly conclusive," Nagumo countered.

"We have also intercepted messages from the American seaplane patrols. By the radio bearings, we are able to fix their position quite accurately. All patrols are still confined to a sector south by southwest of Oahu."

"Are you saying their carriers would be restricted to that sector as well?"

"Yes, sir," Kusaka acknowledged. "Although I believe our original intelligence was correct. Those carriers were assigned to ferry airplanes, not patrol. The Americans suspect nothing."

Nagumo stared out to sea. His expression was somehow inward, as though debating the matter within himself. His eyes were far away, oddly distant.

"So," he finally said, almost to himself. "We entrust ourselves to the German girl after all."

"I beg your pardon, Admiral?"

"Nothing. Order the signal to commence operations."

Signal flags fluttered to the top of the mast and were swiftly lowered. On the other carriers, the order was acknowledged with flags rippling in the wind. Within moments, squadrons of Zero fighter planes roared down the flight decks. High-altitude bombers took off next, followed quickly by Nakajima torpedo planes. The last to thunder off the flight decks were Aichi dive bombers.

Circling overhead, the aircraft slowly converged into three separate formations. Only one plane was lost on take off, and a total of one hundred eighty-three finally wheeled around on a southerly course. A flare of oncoming sunrise brightened the horizon as they winged toward Pearl Harbor. It was 0600.

Admiral Nagumo ordered the second attack division brought

onto the flight decks. While signal flags fluttered, he walked forward on the bridge. His face expressionless, he watched until the first attack wave vanished from sight. Then, almost as an afterthought, he pulled the dispatch from his pocket and read it again. Something odd struck in his mind, and a moment passed before he was able to sort it out. He realized he couldn't remember the German girl's name.

Susan awoke before the alarm went off. She experienced an instant of panic, terrified she'd overslept. Sitting bolt upright, she looked at the clock on the nightstand. It was a few minutes before six-thirty.

Quickly, with a sense of relief, she depressed the alarm button. She had slept fitfully, waking with a start several times throughout the night. But now, scooting out of bed, she told herself it was just as well. Nervous anxiety was preferrable to the strident clamor of an alarm clock. The last thing she wanted was to wake her father.

Her mind was working even as she stepped into her slippers. She would attend to her toilet first thing, while everyone else still slept. That way there was less chance of being discovered awake and about at such an unusually early hour. Afterwards, she would return to her room and dress. She thought something simple, perhaps a skirt and blouse, would be the most practical. A large handbag would allow her to carry everything needed for an overnight stay.

Once dressed, she would remain in her room. At the very earliest, she couldn't expect Harry much before eight-twenty. Yet it was imperative that she be waiting outside the moment he pulled into the driveway. Otherwise she would risk a scene with her father, questions for which she had no explanation. So she planned to wait until the very last moment before leaving her room. Without attracting attention, she would then walk downstairs and straight out the front door. She was determined that no one would stop her.

The house was quiet as doomsday. She made her way to the

bathroom and gently closed the door. When she emerged a short time later, she had every intention of returning to her bedroom. Yet, as she approached the staircase, she felt the pull of some irresistable compulsion. Whatever the reason, she needed reassurance that all was well at Pearl Harbor. She knew it was silly, nothing but nerves, and still she couldn't deny the urge. She had to see for herself.

One step at a time, she went down the stairs. There was an almost ghostly stillness on the ground floor, and she paused a moment in the foyer. Fearful of the least noise, she went past the study and entered the living room. A shaft of sunlight streamed through the open patio door, widening into a fan of gold on the carpet. She was halfway across the room before it registered on her, stopped her short. The patio door was never left open at night.

She moved a step closer, suddenly froze. Her father stood at the edge of the patio, still attired in the suit he'd worn last night. His hands were clasped behind his back and, a pipe jutted from his mouth. One look at his rumpled clothes told her that he hadn't been to bed. The direction of his gaze removed any doubt as to why he was on the patio. He was staring down intently at Pearl Harbor, his stance motionless and curiously rigid. He appeared to be waiting.

Susan turned and fled. Upstairs, she retreated to her bedroom, gingerly closed the door. Her heart was pounding, and the thought foremost in her mind was too terrifying to consider. She asked herself why her father was stationed on the patio at sunrise. Why indeed, unless he'd lied to her about the time of the Japanese attack?

She couldn't bring herself to believe it. For if the attack occurred now, all was lost. No trip to the windward side, no escape for herself or Harry. She looked at the clock and saw the second hand sweeping toward six forty-three. She willed it to move faster, told herself eight o'clock would come and go without incident. And then, just as they'd planned, Harry would take her away.

She forced herself not to think about it. Her hands trembling, she opened the closet and carefully selected an outfit. She began dressing.

A four-man Marine honor guard marched to the flagstaff on the *Nevada*. The ship's band, assembled before them on the fantail, prepared for the colors ceremony. The flag, by tradition, was always raised at eight sharp on Sunday morning.

On the bridge, Bendix watched the preparations with growing impatience. Standing beside him was Lieutenant George Stockman, who would officially relieve him once the colors were raised. But he was unable to leave his post, or the ship, until the ceremony was concluded. He glanced at his watch, noting it was still ten minutes before the hour.

The *Nevada* was moored off the northeast tip of Ford Island. The last ship in line, its berth was directly astern of the *Arizona*. Before them, some moored singly and others positioned side by side, were the remaining dreadnoughts of the fleet. All along the line, honor guard details and bandsmen were gathered on the fantail of every ship. The colors ceremony was one of the few formalities observed on a weekend.

Bendix's gaze was drawn to Halawa Heights. He imagined Susan, waiting there, anxious and frightened. But the thought of seeing her, the certainty of her love, quickly dispelled his concern. He refused to think of tomorrow, or their appointment with Forster. Today was the only day that mattered, their day.

The weather was perfect for a drive to the windward side. Scattered clouds wreathed the mountain peaks, and the sky was an azure infinity. Bendix looked east, where a hot sun slowly crested the slopes of the Koolau Range. Something moved, a silvery glint caught between sun and sky. He shaded his eyes with his hand.

"What do you make of that, Stockman?"

Stockman peered into the sun. The silvery glint separated into distinct shapes, silhouetted now against the mountains. "Looks like planes," Stockman said. "Quite a few of them, too."

A sound caught Bendix's attention. He turned, staring westward, and saw a formation of planes swoop low over the Waianae Range. The planes dropped lower still, hurtling toward the harbor. Out of the corner of his eye, he detected motion to the southwest. Swiveling around, he spotted another formation flying straight up the channel. His features blanched in a look of startled comprehension.

On the fantail, the bandleader gave the downbeat. While the honor guard raised the flag, the band thumped into "The Star-Spangled Banner." An instant later a plane skimmed low across the harbor and dropped a torpedo. There was a splash, then the torpedo surfaced, trailing a white wake as it sped toward the *Arizona*. The plane banked sharply, veering over the *Nevada*, and the rear gunner opened fire with a machine gun. The deck on the fantail splintered as slugs stitched a path from port to starboard. A bright red sun was plainly visible on the plane's wingtips.

Bendix reacted on sheer instinct. He struck an oval brass knob with the palm of his hand and an alarm bell began to clang. Then he grabbed the microphone on the ship's intercom system. His voice boomed out with a whipcrack command.

"General quarters! This is no drill. General quarters! *All hands man battle stations!*"

24

A SHORE PATROL van blocked the driveway. Three cars, following directly behind, braked to a halt at the curb. There was no sign of activity within the house.

Forster stepped from the lead car. The time was 0735 and he was seething with anger. Despite Ordway's call, Lamar Moody hadn't arrived at the base until shortly before seven. His excuse was that he'd needed time to collect a team of agents.

Unconvinced, Forster thought it likely that he'd been on the horn to Washington. Whether or not Hoover had sanctioned the operation would probably never be known. But because of the delay, almost four hours had been consumed in organizing the arrest party. And in Forster's view, it was four hours they could ill afford to lose. He had been hardpressed to restrain his temper.

Their moves now were prearranged. The uniformed Shore Patrol, one officer and three ratings, stationed themselves along the left side of the house. Joe Michaels and his undercover team took the right side, their weapons drawn. Forster and Moody, trailed by three FBI agents, walked straight to the front door. Forster leaned on the buzzer.

Several moments passed in tense silence. Then Hahn opened the door like a man expecting guests. No surprise was evident on his features, and he even managed a wry smile. Moody flashed his identification.

"FBI," he announced. "Are you Dr. Eric Hahn?"

"I am."

"You're under arrest. We also have orders to take your family into custody. The charge is espionage."

Hahn's gaze shifted to Forster. While they had never been formally introduced, each of them knew the other on sight. They stared at one another now in open assessment, like combatants brought face to face. At length, Hahn looked back at Moody.

"I presume you have a warrant?"

Moody brushed him aside. One of the agents took charge of Hahn, while the other two fanned out through the house. Greta was brought from the kitchen, and sequestered with Hahn in the study. A minute or so elapsed before the third agent returned from upstairs, holding Susan firmly by the arm. He bypassed the study and escorted her instead to the living room. Forster was waiting there.

The plan was to interrogate father and daughter separately. Moody had agreed that Forster was the one to question the girl. As she entered the living room, he motioned her to the couch. Not a word was spoken as she obediently moved forward and sat down. Her face was expressionless, and she sat stock-still, staring straight ahead. She couldn't look at him.

Forster's eyes were impersonal. "Susan, I haven't much time. I need some answers and I need them right now."

She still refused to meet his gaze. "What sort of answers?"

"I want to talk to you about Harry Bendix."

Moody seated himself on the edge of the desk. Hahn and Greta occupied the armchairs across from him. One of the agents had frisked Hahn, relieving him of his Walther automatic. Moody examined the pistol a moment, then dropped it into his jacket pocket. He looked at Hahn.

"It's over, Dr. Hahn. We know everything."

"Do you indeed?"

"Yes." Moody's cold eyes drilled into him. "You were followed last night. Our agents witnessed your meeting with Morimura in the dentist's office."

Hahn's smile was ironic, not quite a smirk. "I haven't the faintest idea of what you mean."

"We also know your wife acted as a courier. And your daughter gathered intelligence on Pearl Harbor. We have it all documented — date and time and place."

"Then you have no need of me, do you?"

"Only insofar as loose ends are concerned. One, in particular, I want to ask you about now. What can you tell me about the 'Winds' code?"

Hahn looked genuinely puzzled. "I never heard of it. Why do you ask?"

"You'll gain nothing by playing dumb. We know the Japanese plan to attack Pearl Harbor sometime today. All I'm asking you to tell me is when, the exact hour."

"Even if I knew, why would I tell you?"

"I'll be frank with you, Dr. Hahn. Whatever happens, you're almost certain to get the death sentence. But I might be able to arrange clemency for your wife and daughter."

"In exchange for the time of the attack?"

"Exactly."

Hahn burst out laughing. Greta stared down at the floor with a look of dulled resignation. Somewhat at a loss, Moody waited until Hahn's laughter subsided. His voice was quizzical.

"Are you amused by the thought of death, Dr. Hahn?"

"Not at all."

"Then what's so funny?"

"A private joke," Hahn said blandly, spreading his hands. "Although the humor will become apparent sooner than you expect."

Moody got a sharp sensation of unease. The German had answered him with a riddle, but one purposely simple. The meaning was all too clear. Time was no longer important, or relevant. Time was up.

* * *

"Harry told me you're ready to accept my offer."

"Oh?" Susan forced herself to remain calm. "When was this?"

Forster paused to underscore the words. "Last night . . . before he went aboard his ship."

The reaction was not what he'd expected. Susan raised her head, boldly met his eyes. In that instant, for all the strained circumstances, he was struck again by her poise, her exquisite loveliness. There was something of the enchantress about her even now, some aspect of raw sensuality. He reminded himself that she had not yet turned informant.

"Harry's in danger," he went on. "You knew that last night, didn't you?"

"Did I?"

"You tell me. Why was it so important to get him off the *Nevada?*"

"You seem to have all the answers."

"All but one. We have an ironclad case against you and your father, even your mother. We also know the Japs plan to attack today."

Forster stopped, allowed her to consider the statement. When he resumed, his voice was low and tense. "What we don't know is when they will attack."

"Are you asking me?"

"I'm asking you to save Harry. Or have you changed your mind since last night?"

"No," she said softly, almost to herself. "Last night I thought the attack would come around eleven or so, during church services. Then this morning . . ."

She faltered, her eyes suddenly vacant. Forster pressed her with a note of urgency. "Come on, Susan, don't stop now. What about this morning?"

"I saw father on the patio at sunrise . . . waiting."

"Waiting for the attack to start?"

She shook her head. "I don't know. I'm so confused. I only hoped it wouldn't happen before Harry left his ship."

Forster checked his watch. "It's five till eight, so maybe there's still time. Didn't your father say anything or—"

A distant *whump* reverberated in the morning stillness. The house shook and a lamp on one of the end tables crashed to the floor. Then the sound of explosions, like an ominous string of thunderclaps, filled the room. Fainter, yet somehow piercing, was the shrill whine of airplane engines.

For an instant, Forster and Susan were perfectly still. They seemed frozen in a moment of paralysis, absolute shock. He recovered first, striding rapidly toward the patio door. Only a beat behind, Susan leaped to her feet and followed him from the room. Outside, they halted on the edge of the patio, staring down at a panorama of violence in motion. There was an eerie sense of unreality to the scene.

The sky boiled with warplanes. Torpedo bombers skimmed low over the harbor, seemingly on a collision course with the anchored ships. As their torpedoes churned through the water, the pilots put their planes into a steep climb and streaked aloft. Hurtling downward, dive bombers screamed straight at their targets, like eagles plunging from the sun. Bombs whistled through the air, dropping almost vertically, exploding on impact with a shuddering roar. Torpedoes struck with a muffled *whump*, lifting ships bodily from the water. The intensity of the attack increased as ever more planes savaged the fleet.

The *Arizona* and the *Oklahoma* billowed great clouds of smoke. The *West Virginia* buckled amidships, struck simultaneously by torpedoes at waterline and bombs above decks. All across the harbor, cruisers berthed at docks and destroyers riding at anchor were pummeled relentlessly. But the battle raged fiercest on the leeward side of Ford Island. Wave after wave of planes swarmed and wheeled over Battleship Row, raining down death and destruction. Not one of the fleet's dreadnoughts was still undamaged.

As Susan and Forster watched, a dive bomber nosed downward above the *Arizona*. The plane rocketed through puffs of anti-aircraft fire and pulled up at the very last instant. Dropped from a few hundred feet, the bomb slammed through the ship's forecastle and detonated in the forward powder magazine. The *Arizona* erupted in a titanic explosion, toppling the conning tower and wrenching the forward gun turrets from their mounts. A searing fireball leapt skyward, the vortex a blinding flash of orange and blood-bright gold. Onshore, the force of the blast leveled the northeast tip of Ford Island. Then a thick black mushroom of smoke roiled out of the *Arizona*.

Moored directly astern, the *Nevada* was relatively unscathed. The men on her decks appeared ant-like, some still scurrying to their battle stations. Most of the gun crews were already in action, and anti-aircraft units began peppering the attackers with a steady barrage. Swooping low over the water, a plane suddenly loosed a torpedo off the port bow. An instant later, as dense clouds of smoke rolled leeward from the *Arizona*, the torpedo exploded belowdecks. The *Nevada* vanished from sight.

A strangled scream caught in Susan's throat. She stared down at the carnage in wide-eyed horror, unable to get her breath. As smoke obscured the *Nevada*, her clenched hand went to her mouth and her legs would no longer support her. She slumped limply against Forster.

Holding her upright, he watched in silent rage as the *Arizona* blew apart.

"Engineer!" Bendix shouted into the engine room telephone. The wheelhouse was a wreck, windows shattered and hatches torn loose. His face was streaked with blood, cut by flying shards of glass. He labored for breath as dungeonous clouds of smoke drifted downwind from the *Arizona*. He gripped the telephone tighter.

"Goddamnit, somebody answer me! *Engineer!*"

"Aye," a voice responded. "Who's there?"

"Gunnery Officer Bendix. I've taken the con. Have you got steam?"

"Of sorts, sir. The day boiler was lit at 0600. But I only just came on duty, and I hadn't yet switched the steam load from the night boiler. So we got two pots fired up and cookin'."

"Any chance we can get underway?"

"Yes, sir, a mighty slim chance. I'll have to hustle some bodies down here."

"Then hustle them! When I ring the telegraph, I want full emergency power. Understood?"

"Aye, aye, sir. I'll give 'er the whole load!"

No one questioned Bendix's authority. He was the ranking officer on board, and while he'd never handled the con of a battleship, someone had to assume command. The *Arizona*, by now a blazing hulk, was already settling to the bottom. From his position in the wheelhouse, Bendix looked on with a sense of cold resolve. He was determined the *Nevada* would not go down without a fight. He meant to head for open sea.

The ship, miraculously, had thus far sustained only one serious hit. Belowdecks, within moments after the torpedo struck, the forward compartment had been sealed off. But as the attack intensified, dive bombers swarmed overhead like angry hornets. Their near misses sprayed the decks with water, and Bendix quickly began issuing orders. A work party, led by Lieutenant Stockman, chopped through the hawsers fore and aft with fire axes. The *Nevada* swung clear of her mooring and drifted leeward with the tide.

Bendix cranked the engine room telegraph handles. With a helmsman at the wheel, he reversed engines until the stern nudged the shallows off Ford Island. Then he ordered slow ahead on the starboard engines and hard astern on the port. The bow slowly came around, easing past the burning *Arizona* with only feet to spare. Bendix signaled all ahead on both engines, ordering the helmsman to apply hard right rudder. The fantail, flag fluttering, broke clear of the shallows. The *Nevada* steamed into the channel.

25

LAMAR MOODY RUSHED onto the patio. Behind him, hustling the Hahns along, were the three FBI agents. He stopped beside Forster.

"Too late," he muttered. "Too goddamn late."

Forster, who was still supporting Susan, merely nodded. His eyes were fixed on the harbor and his expression was wooden. He silently cursed himself, overcome by an oppressive sense of guilt. Had he acted sooner, gone directly to Admiral Kimmel, today would never have happened. He wondered what Ordway would say now, and realized it wouldn't matter. There was no absolution after today. Not for himself or Ordway.

The three agents were drawn to the edge of the patio. The Hahns were pushed forward, and everyone stood clustered in a tight group. They stared down, awestruck and silent, mesmerized by the spectacle below the heights. All of Pearl Harbor was ablaze, a watery cauldron. Battleship Row was wreathed in flame and smoke, still under heavy attack. A formation of high altitude bombers appeared from the south, pounding the docks and the Navy Yard. Farther away, Hickam Field burned like a funeral pyre, the grounded American planes, destroyed where they sat. There seemed no end to the carnage.

Susan recovered enough to stand alone. She turned, weeping softly, and allowed herself to be smothered in Greta's arms.

Forster released her, momentarily diverted, and looked around. He saw Hahn standing with military erectness, arms clasped behind his back. His eyes were bright with excitement, darting here and there as the flash of explosions dotted the harbor. A curiously benign smile touched the corners of his mouth.

"Enjoy it!" Forster said bitterly. "It's the last thing you'll ever grin about."

Hahn looked at him with open contempt. "On the contrary, Commander Forster. I daresay I shan't stop laughing for sometime to come."

"Tell it to the hangman. It's hard to laugh with a noose around your neck."

"Indeed? Then I suggest you join me on the gallows, Commander. I will make it a point to have the last laugh — on you."

"Goddamn Nazi," Moody mumbled vehemently.

Hahn wasn't in the least offended. "Why take it personally, Mr. Moody? War is war, and we are, after all, gentlemen."

"Knock it off!" Forster interjected. "All your holier than thou—"

"*Look!* Oh God, look — *there!*"

Susan was rigid, her features attenuated with shock and joy. Forster and the others turned, following the direction of her gaze. Far below, the *Nevada* emerged like a ghost from the pall of smoke. Her guns blazed and chattered as she slowly got underway. Susan choked back a sob, tears flooding her eyes.

Battleship Row was a towering holocaust. Bendix shielded his face from the searing heat. Fire sucked oxygen out of the air and every breath seemed to scorch his lungs. He kept his eyes fastened on the channel, but it was impossible to ignore the tapestry of devastation off Ford Island. Of all the battleships, only the *Nevada* was underway.

The *West Virginia* foundered under the impact of six torpedoes. She began to settle into the mud of the harbor bottom, her main deck awash and still blazing amidships. The *Tennessee*, moored directly inboard, exploded outward, absorbing four bomb hits in rapid succession. The *California* was sinking at the stern, and the *Arizona* lay in ruins. Yet, of all the great dreadnoughts, the tableau of death was most apparent aboard the *Oklahoma*. She took three torpedoes broadside and began to list.

Dead ahead of the *Nevada*, two planes streaked wingtip to wingtip across the harbor. Their torpedoes hammered into the *Oklahoma* even as she started to capsize. While crewmen scrambled for their lives, the ship slowly turned turtle. She rolled onto her port side and kept rolling until the mast and superstructure were bottom down, jammed in the mud. The survivors climbed over the starboard side, balancing like men on a tightwire, and walked with the roll. When the ship bottomed, most of them clung precariously to the hull. Those who jumped or lost their hold were doomed.

The water off Ford Island was a raging inferno. Oil from the stricken ships spewed out and ignited in a solid sheet of flame. Swimming about in a maddened frenzy, the men in the water were quickly coated with burning oil. Charred black, their faces twisted in agony, the sound of their screams rose above the roar of battle. Launches and small boats converged on the ships, braving the firestorm in an effort to rescue the trapped men. But in their wake, machine guns spitting, planes crisscrossed the harbor on deadly strafing runs. The flames licked higher as a maelstrom of bullets shredded men and boats. From shoreline to channel, corpses bobbed on the fiery surface.

Aboard the *Nevada*, Bendix tried to keep his mind from the grisly hell. His attention was distracted as squadrons of high altitude bombers passed over the harbor. Their primary target was the Navy Yard, where ships lay in drydock, and their bombs rained down in a precise checkerboard pattern. The *Pennsylvania*, moved from her mooring off Ford Island only yesterday, shuddered under the impact of a direct hit. Her stern exploded in a shower of debris and twisted steel.

On all sides the *Nevada* was bracketed by death and chaos. Yet Bendix was forced to push it aside, detach himself from the havoc. His one concern was the ship, and ahead lay the major obstacle blocking his path to the sea. A pipeline extended from Ford Island to well past midstream, where it was connected to a dredge. Used to clear the harbor bottom, the dredge was normally towed ashore when battleships got underway. But now, blocking more than half the channel, it reduced maneuvering room to a perilous margin. The slightest error would put the *Nevada* on a collision course with the ships in drydock.

Bendix signaled all ahead slow on the engine room telegraph. He nodded reassuringly to the helmsman and took a position forward in the wheelhouse. His eyes fixed grimly on the dredge.

Susan stared ashen-faced at the *Nevada*. So intense was her concentration that she stepped past Forster without realizing she'd moved. Her hands were clutched to her breast.

Not a word was spoken, and yet Forster read her thoughts perfectly. She believed Bendix was aboard the *Nevada*, still alive. More than that, she saw the ship's passage through the harbor as a prayer answered. Her every instinct told her that Bendix would, after all, escape death.

Forster wasn't so certain. He suspected that Bendix was the ranking officer on board, and therefore at the con of the *Nevada* even now. The odds that an inexperienced gunnery officer could navigate a battleship into open water were less than encouraging. Worse, a moving target attracted attention, invited attack. His instincts told him that Bendix would never make it. He finally broke the silence.

"Time to go, Susan. You can't help him now."

"No, wait," she pleaded. "The ship's slowing down. Why would they do that? I don't understand."

"It's the dredge," Forster pointed out. "He has to reduce speed to get around it. Otherwise, he'd plow straight into the docks."

"He?" Susan looked at him strangely. "Are you saying Harry's in command, running the ship?"

Forster shrugged. "I wouldn't even guess who's in command. Probably whoever got to the bridge first."

"But it could be Harry . . . couldn't it?"

"Anything's possible today. Why, does it make a difference?"

"Yes," she whispered. "I want it to be him. If it is, I just know he'll get away. Somehow he will."

"Maybe he will at that. But we can't wait around—"

Forster's voice trailed off. His gaze went past her, to the harbor. He saw his thought of a moment ago swiftly becoming reality. A light cruiser and two destroyers were steaming down the main channel, headed out to sea. One other ship was underway, the only sign of movement across the breadth of Pearl Harbor. And it was apparent that the ship had at last drawn attention from the attackers. Every plane in the sky seemed to turn and suddenly descend on the *Nevada*.

Susan screamed. Her mouth ovaled in terror and she involuntarily moved toward the patio railing. Forster took her arm, spun her around. "Come on, let's go. I've seen enough."

"Please, John," she begged. "Please let me stay. I have to know!"

"Whether you stay or not won't change a thing. Don't argue with me, Susan. I have to get back to the base—right now."

"I won't go! Oh God, John, *please!*"

Forster motioned to one of the FBI agents. The man stepped forward and caught hold of Susan's arms. She struggled and fought, tears streaking her face as he lifted her bodily and carried her from the patio. The other agents, followed by Moody, escorted the Hahns through the door. Forster delayed a moment, took one last look at the harbor. The *Nevada* appeared wreathed in airplanes. He silently wished Bendix luck.

The helmsman gingerly played the wheel. Bendix watched intently as the dredge loomed off the starboard bow. To avoid the docks, he would have to negotiate a lazy hairpin curve around the dredge. He calculated the *Nevada* would squeeze through with only yards to spare.

In the drydocks, the destroyer *Shaw* suddenly blew up with a spectacular burst. Hit forward by a heavy bomb, the powder magazines exploded and tore away the ship's bow. A monstrous fireball flung bodies into the water and scattered debris like roman candles jetting skyward. The force of the blast rocked the *Nevada* and for a moment the battleship lost headway. Then she swung gently to port, entering the hairpin curve.

Bendix caught movement out of the corner of his eye. He looked around as a wave of torpedo planes swept in off the starboard quarter. For an instant, even as the antiaircraft batteries unleashed a fearsome barrage, he thought the *Nevada* would be struck broadside. But the planes zoomed past, their rear gunners raking the decks with machine gun fire. He dimly realized that none of them had dropped torpedoes.

Off the stern, a squadron of dive bombers hurtled downward. The machine guns mounted in their wings winked orange flashes, and slugs splintered the decks from fantail to forecastle. Yet, with a slow-moving target dead in their sights, no bombs fell. For the next few minutes, the sky above the *Nevada* boiled with planes. Wave after wave attacked, machine guns spitting as they roared in from every direction. And slowly, almost unbelievingly, it dawned on Bendix why there were no bombs, no torpedoes. The planes had already dropped their payloads, expended their main armament. They were reduced now to strafing runs.

The attack stopped with dizzying suddenness. One moment there was the shriek of engines, the deadly rattle of gunfire, and in the next there was deafening silence. As though on command, the planes abruptly wheeled away from Pearl Harbor, gaining altitude. After joining up in ragged formations, they winged westward toward the mountains. Here and there, stragglers made a final strafing run. The last plane buzzed low over the destroyers anchored in the northern quadrant. The pilot derisively wig-wagged his wings.

Bendix watched as the plane went into a steep climb and banked sharply above Halawa Heights. A fleeting image of Susan passed through his mind, then was quickly gone. He once more turned his attention to the dredge, and the open sea beyond. His mouth lifted in a tight, razored smile. He knew he would make it now.

Outside the house, Forster took Moody aside. They talked in subdued tones a minute, debating what should be done with the Hahn family. Lodging them in the Pearl Harbor brig was clearly out of the question.

The FBI agents stood with Joe Michaels's undercover team on the lawn. The Shore Patrol detail waited near the van, which still blocked the driveway. All the men were solemn-faced and quiet, staring intently at the billowing clouds of smoke over Pearl Harbor. As the sounds of battle abruptly ceased, they saw formations of planes flying westward. Shielding their eyes, they stared upward with a mixture of puzzlement and surprise. None of them quite believed it was over.

The Hahns stood in a tight knot beneath the banyan tree. Greta looked wistfully at the house, while Hahn watched the departing planes. Susan appeared beaten, even though she'd regained a measure of composure. After being dragged out of the house, she had simply stopped resisting, too weak to fight. But a spark of hope still burned within her, fanned brighter now by an apparent end to the attack. She clung desperately to the belief that he was alive, safe aboard the *Nevada*. She refused to accept the alternative.

Forster motioned to the Shore Patrol officer. "Lieutenant, I'm placing you under Mr. Moody's command. You'll escort the prisoners to the Honolulu jail and see that they're locked up."

"Aye, aye, sir."

Forster turned back toward the house. His gaze touched on Susan a moment, quickly shifted to her father. "Dr. Hahn, I want you and your family to get in the van. Please be quick about it."

Hahn shrugged, exchanging a look with Greta. He started across the lawn and Susan fell in beside her mother. One of the Shore Patrol ratings hurried to open the rear doors on the van.

An *Aichi* bomber suddenly crested Halawa Heights some distance down the street. The plane banked sharply to port, and the pilot immediately spotted uniforms and a military van. He leveled off not ten feet above the housetops and roared toward the cul de sac. Halfway down the block, he opened fire with his wing guns.

The grassy lawn spurted clouds of sod. A dull pock-pock-pock sound filled the air as tracer slugs stitched a path across the yard. The men along the curb dove for cover behind their vehicles. Forster and Moody hit the ground, and the Shore Patrol detail scattered. Hahn scooped Greta into his arms and flung her down behind the tree. Susan ran for the Cadillac.

The plane thundered over the house as she jumped into the car. The key was in the ignition, where her father always left it, and she hit the starter button. Hooking the gearshift into reverse, she backed out of the driveway, swerving around the van, and bumped over the curb. She slammed the brake and spun the steering wheel, straightening the car out as it jolted to a stop. Then she jammed into low gear and screeched off in a haze of burning rubber. The Cadillac accelerated as she speed-shifted and put the gas pedal to the floorboard.

She drove toward the swirling tower of smoke over Pearl Harbor.

26

THE SHORE PATROL van was only a block behind. Susan saw it in her rearview mirror. At the bottom of Halawa Heights, she tore through the intersection without braking. A horn blared and she swerved to avoid hitting a car in the crosslane. She automatically glanced back, caught a glimpse of the van approaching the intersection. She kept her foot on the floorboard.

Some inner voice told her it was Forster. While the distance was too great to make out the driver, she was nonetheless gripped by certainty. Forster would never have entrusted pursuit to someone else. He was behind the wheel of the van, and clearly determined to overtake her. She was just as determined not to be overtaken.

What she hoped to accomplish wasn't clear. She hadn't paused to think it through when the Japanese plane strafed the yard. She'd merely reacted, seizing the opportunity to escape. A compulsion too visceral to identify pulled her toward Pearl Harbor. Harry Bendix was there and it seemed important that she get there too. The fact that she might not see him, probably wouldn't get anywhere near the *Nevada*, was something she refused to consider. She had to try.

The base was on her right, west of the road. Ford Island, and much of the naval shipyard, was obscured by smoke. But the southern quadrant of the harbor, off the tip of Ford Island, was plainly visible. She saw the *Nevada* execute a slow turn to starboard, barely moving as it eased past some sort of barge. The ship appeared undamaged, and the sky was empty of planes. Her hopes soared, and she quickly checked the rearview mirror. The van was still there.

Suddenly her heart almost stopped. A short distance down the road she saw a snarled traffic jam outside the main gate. Scores of taxicabs loaded with sailors, and hundreds of private cars, were backed up bumper to bumper. The road from Honolulu, where thousands of men had been caught on weekend shore leave, was virtually impassable. Ahead of Susan, on the road skirting the Makalapa district, a long line of cars was inching along. The bottleneck at the main gate got worse with each passing moment. And the van was drawing ever closer.

Forster's jaws were clenched tight with anger. He felt the fool for allowing her to escape, and his rage was directed more at himself than Susan. But as she slowed for the traffic jam, he swiftly closed the gap. He told himself the chase was about to end.

Abruptly, like a madwoman possessed, she took to the shoulder of the road. Sparks flew as the Cadillac bounced off the chain link fence bordering the perimeter of the base. For a moment, jouncing and swaying, she almost lost control of the car. Then she got the wheels straightened out and went tearing down the shoulder. She roared toward the bottleneck at the main gate.

Forster cursed out loud. He braked hard, fearful of rolling the top-heavy van, and eased off onto the shoulder. As he accelerated, he began passing cars at the rear of the line. One of them looked familiar, and as he swept by he recognized Admiral Ordway's personal car. In the sideview mirror, he saw Ordway pull out of line and swing onto the shoulder. He wondered why the admiral hadn't taken to the shoulder before now, and the answer almost made him laugh. Ordway had never had an original idea in his life.

A glint in the sky attracted Forster's attention. He glanced eastward and saw a formation of some seventy or eighty dive bombers winging toward Pearl Harbor. He swore savagely, pounding the steering wheel with his fist. But in the next instant he forgot the fleet and began worrying about himself. A wave of Zero fighter planes, until now flying escort for the bombers, peeled off and hurtled earthward. Several pilots, looking for targets of opportunity, spotted the traffic jam. Their wing guns chattering, they dove on the main gate.

The first Zero made a south to north strafing run. Forster ducked his head as the plane barreled straight at the van. A slug shattered the windshield and blew the stuffing out of the passenger seat. Automatically, as the Zero swept past, he glanced in the sideview mirror. The hood of Ordway's car seemed to disintegrate, and a tongue of fire leaped out as a tracer hit the fuel line. A split second later the gas tank exploded and Ordway was hurled against the dashboard. The entire car burst into flame.

Forster jerked his eyes away from the mirror. He looked up at the exact moment Susan slammed through the fence where it joined the main gate. A Marine guard threw his rifle to his shoulder and fired as the Cadillac caromed off a car pulling away from the guard hut. The bullet ricocheted off the trunk and imploded the rear window. The Cadillac sped on toward the harbor. Forster blasted through the gate a moment later.

The *Nevada* eased into the last turn. Bendix watched intently as the dredge slipped past the starboard bow. He was so absorbed in the maneuver that he heard the bombs before he saw the planes. His head snapped around.

Off the port side, the drydocks erupted in flames. The destroyers *Cassin* and *Downes*, berthed ahead of the *Pennsylvania*, were ripped apart. The *Cassin* capsized, rolling heavily to starboard, and crashed into the *Downes*. A huge ball of fire embraced both ships, and the drydocks arched skyward in a convulsive explosion. The shock wave rippled outward with cyclonic force.

Fists clenched, Bendix silently damned the Jap pilots. Yet, despite himself, he felt a grudging sense of admiration. A lull, not unlike the eye of a hurricane, had settled over Pearl Harbor following the initial onslaught. And now, perfectly timed, the second wave had achieved yet another surprise attack. It was shrewdly planned, brilliantly executed.

Collecting himself, Bendix signaled all ahead full on the engine telegraph. He was vaguely aware of the muffled bark of pom-pom guns, and he saw a Jap bomber explode in midair, crash into the harbor. Beyond, on the southwestern tip of Ford Island, he noted PBY seaplanes burning like papier-mâché toys. But his concentration was focused on Hospital Point, only a quarter-mile off the port bow. There, overlooked by the base hospital, lay the entrance to the ocean channel. With only a few minutes reprieve, the *Nevada* would be on her way to open sea. He told himself it was still possible.

Then, like a nightmare revisited, every plane in the sky seemingly fixed on the *Nevada*. From all across the harbor, wave after wave swooped downward in attack. When the bombs struck, kettledrum thunder reverberated throughout the ship. Four direct hits forward were followed by a rumbling explosion from belowdecks. Fires raged amidships, and within minutes the *Nevada* listed ominously to port. Severe flooding was reported in the forward compartments, water pouring through a ruptured bulkhead. The Damage Control Officer estimated the hole was too large to offset with counterflooding. He warned that the ship was in imminent danger of sinking.

Another hit forward decided it for Bendix. If the *Nevada* was sunk in the channel entrance, then what remained of the Pacific Fleet would be bottled up in the harbor. He looked seaward, wishing it might have ended differently. But he knew, however reluctant the admission, that only one command was possible. He ordered the *Nevada* beached on Hospital Point.

The helmsman spun the wheel toward shore. When Bendix ordered the engines stopped, the current caught the stern and swung the ship completely around. He watched helplessly as the stern was driven aground in the shallows and the bow came to rest partially submerged in deep water. For a moment, he feared the current would set her adrift and pull her under in the channel. But the stern held fast, mired in the bottoms only a few feet from the shoreline. He quickly ordered the boilers shut down.

With a sudden jolt, the entire ship seemed to broach violently in the water. A bomb gutted the forecastle and another direct hit tore through the bridge. The superstructure lifted skyward, cleaved apart by the explosion. The wheelhouse simply vanished in a flash of molten brilliance. Like volcanic ash, rubble rained down across Hospital Point. The *Nevada* settled still and dead in the shallows.

Susan pushed the speedometer past seventy. She was tracking the *Nevada*, roaring across the base on a road immediately south of the shipyard. The only traffic she encountered was a lone ambulance. She overtook it like a bullet in flight.

On her right, the shipyards resembled a gigantic bonfire. Cruisers and destroyers berthed there were ablaze, burning out of control. Fireboats stood offshore, spouting jets of water that scarcely dampened the flames. Across the harbor, Battleship Row was a dense pall of smoke, blotting out Ford Island. Devastation of the great dreadnoughts appeared total.

The car was suddenly rocked by a scorching blast. Susan gasped, momentarily stunned as the drydocks seemed to leap from the earth. Looking beyond the ships docked there, she saw the *Nevada* steam into the mouth of the ocean channel. Her heartbeat quickened, and an electric surge of relief shot through her body. But in the next instant her eyes went round with terror.

Japanese dive bombers swarmed over the *Nevada*. The sky above blossomed with dusty puffs as the antiaircraft batteries opened fire. Susan wheeled around a corner, dimly aware of the base hospital a couple of blocks ahead. Out of the side window, she watched horror-stricken as the *Nevada* shuddered under several direct hits. She almost ran off the road but quickly recovered, gripping the steering wheel so hard her knuckles turned white. When she looked back, the ship had begun to lose headway.

Slowing down, she saw the bow of the *Nevada* come around, angled toward Hospital Point. It passed through her mind that the ship was crippled, unable to make speed or navigate properly. But whatever the cause, it was clear that the *Nevada* was about to run aground. She braked hard, rounding a corner as an ambulance went past her in the opposite direction. A short distance ahead was the hospital complex, three brick buildings on direct line with the harbor entrance. She gunned the motor, rapidly picking up speed, and drove on.

Beyond the hospital, a grove of trees extended to the shoreline. The *Nevada's* superstructure was visible above the trees, and Susan thought something looked oddly out of place. Staring closer, she realized the ship had rotated in a complete arc, running aground by the stern. A sudden flash of light almost blinded her as the superstructure detonated with an ear-splitting roar. She gagged a silent scream and her features distorted in a shapeless grimace. High above the trees, she saw twisted shards of steel and something else—bodies—floating down in an eerie, curiously tranquil, sort of slow motion.

Outside the hospital, she skidded to a stop and jumped from the car. She ran with mindless panic, all thought suspended, dodging and weaving through the trees. By the time she reached the shoreline, nurses and medics from the hospital were pulling bodies from the water. Some of the crew were horribly mangled, arms and legs missing, bloody lumps of rag and splintered bone. Others were charred black, steaming the sickly-sweet odor of burnt flesh. She choked back the bile in her throat, hurried from body to body in mounting desperation. Then she saw him.

A uniformed medic was crouched beside Bendix. Her face went slack with fear as she watched him vainly trying for a pulse. She dropped to her knees, staring down with a look of desolate anguish. Bendix was scorched terribly across his arms and upper body. His eyebrows were singed off and wisps of smoke curled from his hair. Sticky red blood trickled from a gash in his forehead that laid the bone bare. She looked up, found a shred of voice.

"Is he all right?"

"Hard to say," the medic mumbled. "Got a real weak pulse."

"Will he live?"

"You his wife?"

Her voice rose shrilly. "*Answer me!* Will he live?"

The medic frowned, slowly shook his head. He stood and moved quickly to a man attempting to crawl from the shallows. Susan put her arms beneath Bendix, lifted him gently and cushioned his head on her breast. Somewhere deep inside she took strength, pulled herself together. She softly spoke his name.

"Harry. Oh, Harry, please—please don't . . ."

Bendix stirred. His eyes rolled open and he stared up at her with a look of groggy recognition. "Susan."

"Yes, darling, it's me. I'm here. I won't leave you."

"Hope not. You still my girl?"

"Only yours, always. I promise."

"God, you're gorgeous . . . always were."

"Just hold on, don't talk. We'll get you a doctor."

A smile shadowed his mouth. "Quit worrying. I've still got lots . . ."

His voice stopped in a sharp outrush of breath. Suddenly his head lolled sideways and he went limp in her arms. His lips were still parted in a smile.

Tears flooded her eyes. A strange expression came over her face, and she bent down, cupping his chin in her hand. She kissed him tenderly on the mouth.

Forster halted at the edge of the treeline. He watched as she kissed Bendix, then hugged him to her breast. The moans of the wounded and dying, the smoldering hulk of the *Nevada*, were like a world apart. He couldn't take his eyes off Susan.

She looked up, as though sensing his stare. Her face was streaked with tears, and her expression was empty. For a long moment she simply returned his gaze. Then she nodded, smiling faintly, and something unspoken passed between them. He understood that there was no deliverance for her, no absolution. Now, even in her own mind, there was only judgment. Her life ended here.

High above the *Nevada*, a lone plane appeared in the sky. Forster threw up his arms in warning, called out her name as the pilot nosed downward in a steep dive. She turned, looking over her shoulder, still clutching Bendix in her arms. While nurses and medics scattered for cover, she watched the plane swoop low past the ship. Her eyes fastened on the bomb, dropped too late. She stared upward as it whistled across the stern of the *Nevada* and bore straight at the beach. She waited, her expression serene and without fear. She looked at peace. At the last instant, Forster took cover behind the trees.

A fiery blast shook the ground, hurling rocks and shrapnel across the landscape. Where the bomb exploded, there was now a blackened crater several feet deep. Heavy gray smoke drifted inland, borne along by a breeze thick with the odor of cordite. Forster waited until the smoke cleared, then climbed to his feet. He stepped from the trees and started forward, suddenly stopped. His face froze in a harrowed look.

Susan lay sprawled on the beach. One arm was outflung, reaching even now toward Bendix. Neither of them moved.

27

SHE AWOKE IN drowsy stages. Her eyelids felt lead-weighted, and her head throbbed with a dull ache. For several moments, when she first opened her eyes, there was a giddy sensation of vertigo. As the dizziness faded, her vision slowly cleared.

Somewhat disoriented, she looked around the room. Sunlight filtered dimly through venetian blinds covering a window. Everything seemed curiously sterile, almost antiseptic. The walls were a perfect match with the snowy bed linen and her white smock. She suddenly realized she was in a hospital.

It all came back to her in a sickening rush. She got a sharp image of those last moments on the beach. Harry dead in her arms, and Forster calling out her name, motioning frantically. The plane swooping past, then the bomb falling gracefully from the sky. Her final instant of acceptance, welcoming death. And now . . .

She was alive. So far as she could tell, she wasn't even seriously injured. Her vision blurred and tears spilled down her cheeks. It seemed unfair, somehow unpardonable. All she'd wanted was to die, let it end swiftly and without complication. She felt cheated.

A nurse marched into the room. She was pleasant, efficiently brisk, and genuinely delighted to find Susan awake. Hovering over the bed, she popped a thermometer into Susan's mouth and took her pulse. All the while she kept up a cheery monologue, meant to reassure and inform. Susan had sustained a concussion, nothing to cause permanent damage. Aside from intermittent delirium, she'd been unconscious for the last twenty-four hours. It was now Monday morning, and to Susan's question, she replied, "Why, yes, of course. You're in the base hospital."

Shortly, a doctor stopped by to examine Susan. He pronounced her in remarkably good condition, noting she'd been a "very lucky young lady." The nurse returned with broth and hot tea, even cheerier after the doctor's report. She gave Susan a sponge bath, changed her into a fresh smock, and brushed her hair until it shone. When Susan was finally allowed to rest, she lay back on her pillow, vaguely troubled. Neither the doctor nor the nurse had called her by name. She wondered why.

Forster arrived late that morning. He entered the room carrying a large manila envelope, carefully closed the door. His manner, somewhat reserved and formal, suggested that it was not a personal visit. Yet his tone was gentle, even considerate.

"You gave us a scare. I'm glad to see you're feeling better."

Susan turned her head into the pillow. "It's kind of you to say so, after yesterday."

"About that—" Forster halted beside the bed, looking down at her. "Let me bring you up to date. We have your family in custody, and of course, we've arrested everyone at the Japanese consulate. For the moment, we're holding you incommunicado."

"What possible difference does it make?"

"Perhaps a great deal. As a matter of fact, your name was listed among the civilian dead in this morning's paper. You might say you no longer exist."

She looked up, strangely puzzled. "Why?"

Forster opened the manila envelope. He dumped her father's intelligence journal and three passports onto the bed. "When we searched the house, we found these hidden in your father's desk. The journal pretty much speaks for itself. I assume the phony passports were meant for an emergency—correct?"

"Yes," she said dismally. "We were given a contact in New York. If things went wrong, we were to travel there and he would have arranged our passage to South America. Eventually, we would have returned to Germany."

"Who's the contact?"

"A man named Ernst Jahnke."

"Do you know anything about him?"

"Father insisted on a thorough briefing before we left Berlin. He was told Jahnke operates an espionage network along the Eastern Seaboard."

Forster thought for a moment. "After we found the passports, I contacted Washington. Last night our intelligence people and the FBI got their heads together. I've been authorized to offer you a deal."

"Pardon me?"

"A trade-off. You agree to turn double agent, work for us. Officially, you're dead, and that ought to make you even more valuable to Jahnke. It shouldn't be too difficult to infiltrate his entire operation. Once you're set, you'll start reporting to the FBI."

"And what do I receive in the trade?"

"Your father's life. Normally, he'd be tried and executed in no time flat. We'll agree to a sentence of life imprisonment."

"Why should I want to save my father?"

Forster stared at her with some surprise. "Why wouldn't you?"

"Because he lied." There was a terrible desolation in her voice. "Everything I planned went wrong because he lied about the time of the attack. And now Harry's . . . ."

"No," Forster said, watching her anguished features. "Harry's not dead."

She looked deep into his eyes. "I don't believe you."

"It's true. By all rights, he should be dead twice over. I guess some men just aren't meant to be killed. Harry Bendix is one of them."

"But his wounds—"

"Bad," Forster nodded. "I wouldn't kid you about that. It'll be a long time before he walks the deck of a ship. But he's not going to die."

Her eyes flooded with tears. She thought her heart would burst, and a magical wonderment came over her face. She finally managed a whisper. "Why haven't you told me . . . before now?"

"Well, I sort of sold Washington on the idea of a double agent. So I had to have something to trade besides your father. Harry seemed like the best bet."

"And if I agree? What happens then?"

"The doctor says you'll be able to travel in a few days. Your phony passport will get you to New York, and Jahnke."

"You've answered only part of the question. What about Harry?"

"I guess that's up to you and Harry—after the war's over."

She considered briefly, then nodded. "Will I be allowed to see him before I leave?"

"No," Forster said firmly. "Too many people on the base know you. Some of them are patients here right now."

"But surely you could arrange—"

"Sorry. We just can't risk having you spotted. Except for your doctor and a handful of nurses, you're the invisible woman. Susan Hahn is dead and buried and forgotten. I suggest you get used to the idea."

"It won't be easy, but I'll try."

"Good. Get some rest and we'll talk later."

Collecting the journal and passports, Forster turned toward the door. Her voice stopped him. "John."

"Yes?"

"How will Harry know I'm alive?"

Forster looked oddly embarrassed. He attempted to hide it behind a gruff tone. "I've already told him. But just him—nobody else!"

"Thank you, John . . . for everything."

"Don't mention it."

She snuggled deeper into her pillow. The door closed behind him, and yet his words still rang in her ears. *Dead and buried and forgotten.* She smiled. It seemed fitting, somehow appropriate. The perfect epitaph for Susan Hahn.

* * *

Forster walked to the end of the hall. He entered a spacious, sundrenched room normally reserved for flag officers. Bendix was asleep. A large window looked north across Pearl Harbor. Quietly, Forster moved past the bed, halted at the window. His eyes narrowed as he stared at the devastation. Three battleships, along with some 2,000 officers and men, had been lost. The other dreadnoughts, according to early estimates, were thought to be salvageable.

Even the *Nevada*, still aground on Hospital Point, would be refloated and returned to service. Whether fluke or miracle, no other ships had been sunk. Some were damaged extensively, but none were beyond repair. Cruisers and destroyers, the entire submarine pack, were operational.

Suddenly attentive, Forster watched as the *Enterprise* steamed into the harbor. The carrier reduced speed and slowly maneuvered towards its mooring off Ford Island. He stared out the window, smiling inwardly, exhilarated by the sight. He thought it an omen, a peephole into the future. The Japs hadn't seen the last of the Pacific Fleet.

"What's so interesting out there?"

Forster turned back to the bed. Bendix looked uncannily like a fresh-wrapped mummy. He was swathed in bandages, only his mouth and eyes visible. Apart from the head wounds, his principal injury was burns suffered in the wheelhouse explosion. Morphine deadened the pain, causing him to drift in and out of consciousness. He appeared remarkably alert now.

"The *Enterprise*," Forster replied, moving to the bed. "She's just entering the harbor."

"Wish to hell I could say the same."

"Quit bitching! You're almost certain to get the Navy Cross—"

"Big deal," Bendix mumbled through the bandages.

"—and I'll be damned surprised if you aren't promoted to Commander. The way you handled the *Nevada* was worth the price of admission. You're something of a legend around here, Harry."

"Stow the soft soap and tell me about Susan. Has she come out of it yet?"

"As a matter of fact, we just had a long talk. She's fine, no aftereffects at all. So you can stop worrying."

"Did she ask about me?"

Forster nodded. "I explained the situation. She's not happy, but she accepts my reasons. I suggest you follow her example."

"Christ!" Bendix grumbled. "You still won't tell me what's happening. Why all the secrecy?"

"No can do," Forster said quickly. "Come on, cheer up, Harry. The war won't last forever."

"You're all heart, Forster."

"She's willing to wait. She told me so herself."

"When you see her—" Bendix hesitated, his eyes suddenly moist behind the bandages. "Well, hell, you know what to tell her. Just say it's from me."

"Harry?"

"Yeah."

"For what it's worth, you've got great taste in women. She's a gutsy little gal."

Forster went out quickly. Bendix stared at the door for a long time. Then his eyes closed and the image of her leaped vividly to mind. He heard her voice, tasted again the honeyed sweetness of her lips. He slept without pain.

On Friday Kathryn and Forster drove out to Diamond Head. They parked on a turnout overlooking the rocky palisade of Kuilei Cliffs. Far below, the opalescent waters were bounded by a seemingly infinite horizon. Kathryn watched as a sea gull veered slowly into the wind, reminded somehow of a feathered sculpture in flight. Beside her, Forster looked out across the ocean, squinting against a bright noonday sun. She was acutely aware that he was in one of his quiet moods, apparently lost in thought. Neither of them had spoken more than a few words on the way from the house.

Opening the door, Kathryn got out and walked to the guard

rail at the edge of the cliffs. She had no idea why he'd called, suggesting they take a drive. But she welcomed the diversion, any excuse to leave the house. She'd come to think of it as a mausoleum since her father's death. Still, her sorrow was tempered by the knowledge that they would soon be married. Forster agreed there was no reason for prolonged mourning, and they had already set a wedding date. She wondered now why they'd bothered to postpone it at all. With war raging across the Pacific, she wished it were tomorrow, or better yet, today. Time suddenly seemed to her a very precious thing.

Forster watched her from the car. He was sensitive to her grief, and for reasons of his own, he too regretted her father's death. He'd realized the full extent of his loss only last Monday, when Roosevelt addressed Congress, requesting a declaration of war. At the time, he had been struck by the opening line of the President's speech: "Yesterday, December 7, 1941, a date which will live in infamy . . ." Forster thought the greater infamy had died with Admiral Thomas Ordway.

Washington was certain to order an investigation into the attack. But with Ordway dead, there was nothing to be gained in postmortem accusations. Forster had already decided to say nothing about his repeated warnings, the countless signals foreshadowing Japan's attack on the Pacific Fleet. In an effort to cover themselves, the brass would close ranks, whitewash the whole affair. A lone intelligence officer, attempting to cast blame on a dead man, would merely present them with the perfect scapegoat. So he would bring no charges against Ordway, and the world would never hear the truth. Pearl Harbor need not have happened.

Below, Forster saw a passenger liner hove into view. Scheduled to depart at noon, it was now clear of the Honolulu waterfront, bound for Los Angeles. He waited while the ship steamed toward Diamond Head, slowly gathering speed. When it was directly opposite Kuilei Cliffs, he gathered a pair of naval binoculars from the back seat and stepped out of the car. Kathryn turned as he approached, looking at him curiously. He extended the binoculars.

"Don't ask questions," he said quietly. "Just zero in on that ship. Have a look at the promenade deck."

Kathryn caught an odd note in his voice. She took the binoculars and dutifully turned back seaward. The ship was a short distance offshore, quartering away into deep water. She adjusted the focus, and the powerful lenses brought every detail into sharp relief. She swept the promenade deck, then suddenly stopped, the binoculars locked amidships. A delicate figure dressed in mauve sprang into view.

"Oh — my — God! She's *alive!*"

Kathryn swung around, lowering the binoculars. Her face was ablaze with excitement, her eyes wide and round. Forster stared out to sea, saying nothing. All the more bemused, she took another look through the binoculars, laughing happily. The ship slowly altered course onto a north by northeast heading.

"Why didn't you tell me — ?" Kathryn grabbed him around the neck, peppered him with kisses. "She's alive and you let her go. You let Susan go!"

Forster's expression revealed nothing. "Think what you want. Only think it to yourself, and never say it out loud. I'd hate to be drummed out of the service because of a gabby wife."

"Aren't you the sly dog!" Her eyes took on a knowing, madcap gleam. "Susan's working for you, isn't she? Some hush-hush, sealed-lips sort of assignment. And don't you dare lie to me. I'm right, aren't I?"

"Let's just say she's seen the light, and let it go at that."

"And Harry Bendix? Tell me she hasn't lost him — not for good."

"Kate — " Forster hesitated, threw her a quick, enigmatic glance. "I'll tell you exactly what I told Harry. 'The war won't last forever.' Anything else, you'll have to decipher for yourself."

Kathryn gave him a broad, conspiratorial wink. In spite of himself, he laughed, the wooden expression replaced by a grin.

He put his arm around her waist and she nestled her head against his shoulder. Standing there in a bright pool of sunlight, they looked down once more from the cliffs. Their thoughts went out to the ship, and the girl. Forster silently wished her Godspeed.

Susan stood at the railing on the promenade deck. Far astern she could still see the Aloha Tower at the municipal wharves. She took a last look at Waikiki and the emerald slopes of the mountains. Off the port side, Diamond Head loomed against an azure sky.

All around her, passengers crowding the deck were tossing their leis into the water. Hawaiian legend held that if the lei floated inland it foretold a person would return to the islands. Like the others, she'd had several garlands looped around her neck as she boarded ship. But she wasn't tempted to throw even a single strand overboard. She knew she would never return to Hawaii.

A man standing nearby eyed her with an appreciative smile. She wore a silk shantung dress with a mandarin collar and full sleeves. The bodice was pleated, curving softly over her breasts, and a shaped belt accented her stem waist. She'd chosen the dress with care, for mauve was her favorite color and she needed something to cheer her mood. She studiously ignored the man's stare.

From Diamond Head, a reflection of sunlight on glass caught her eye. She looked closer and saw a car parked on the turnout above the cliffs. Visible, but somewhat less distinct, were the figures of a man and woman. The man was dressed in white, what appeared to be the uniform of a naval officer. A fleeting montage passed through her mind, memories and sharp images. All those nights at the Officers' Club. The gaiety and laughter of Kathryn. Even Forster, who in his own way had proved to be her friend. And Harry Bendix.

She regretted many things. The thought of her mother in prison filled her with remorse. As for her father, she forgave him nothing. The one consolation was that, through him, she'd ultimately, magically, found Harry. She wished a farewell had been possible, even a few words, Harry's arms about her, one last kiss. But the exigencies of war made no allowance for lovers. Secrecy and her new mission had taken priority over all else.

Early that morning, she'd been spirited out of the hospital, and into a waiting taxi. The driver was an FBI agent, and he had handed over her stateroom tickets as well as a large sum of cash. Her clothes and jewelry, neatly packed in a steamer trunk, had been brought from the house on Halawa Heights. At the wharf, she had boarded ship with throngs of civilians and mainland tourists, all fleeing Hawaii. She'd felt very much alone at the time, almost fugitive. And she felt even more the expatriate now. America seemed a great unknown, so distant.

"Good morning, Miss Osborn."

The man standing beside her smiled and tipped his hat. Startled, it took a moment for the name to register on her. The name on her phony passport, her new name. Helen Osborn. She recovered quickly, assumed the role with practiced ease. A captivating smile touched her lips.

"You must excuse me. I've such a dreadful memory for faces. Have we met?"

"Only indirectly. We have a mutual friend at Pearl Harbor."

"Oh, yes, of course! I was told I might be contacted. Although I must confess, your name slips my mind."

"Paul Hughes," he said, lowering his voice. "I'll act as your companion on the voyage. To all appearances, we'll strike up a shipboard romance."

"How clever," she observed coolly. "I trust it will be just that—an act."

"Strictly business. I'm here to brief you, nothing more. Contacts, safe houses, dead drops. Everything you'll need in New York."

"In that event, we should get along famously . . . Paul."

"Perhaps we could meet for a drink later. The main lounge, around fiveish?"

"Certainly. Our first tête-à-tête. A marvelous idea."

Susan smiled graciously. He tipped his hat and strolled aft along the deck. She watched him a moment, impressed by his quiet air of assurance. The thought occurred that it wouldn't be so bad working with the Americans after all. She suddenly felt comfortable with the assignment, eager to test herself against a professional spymaster such as Jahnke. Then, too, she had a vested interest in bringing down the Nazis. Once the Third Reich fell, Japan would not be far behind.

Her heart spoke to her. Beyond stretched the luminous expanse of the ocean, and only good lay ahead. Some deep, intuitive sense told her there was nothing illusory in what she dreamed. One day soon the war would end and then . . . then there would be time for love. A lifetime.

If you have enjoyed this book and would like to receive
details of other Walker adventure titles,
please write to:

Adventure Editor
Walker and Company
720 Fifth Avenue
New York, NY 10019